Twisted Mary 2
The Beginning of The End

Twisted Mary 2
The Beginning of The End

BY

TRACY WILSON

http://beautifulpublications.com

Published by
Beautiful Publications LLC
Stratford, CT 06614

PRINT ISBN: 978-1-7331792-5-6
EBOOK ISBN: 978-1-7334002-5-1

Printed in the United States of America

Dedication

I dedicate this series to all the women that were given second chances and smart enough to take them.

Chapter 1

Chandler woke up first, got up, and went to the bathroom.... "Hmmm... it's 7 a.m...." Chandler said as he got back in bed... "Starr..." he whispered as he massaged her breasts. Starr moved a bit but didn't open her eyes... "Starr..." Chandler whispered as he got up, spread Starr's legs, and laid down on top of her...

"Hmmm?" Starr answered sleepily...

"Wake up..." he whispered as he kissed her... "So I can give you dessert..." he breathed as he eased himself inside her and started thrusting...

"Oh... Chandler..." Starr moaned...

"Yes... Starr..." Chandler breathed as he continued thrusting...

"Chandler... wait..."

"No..." Chandler breathed...

"Chandler... wait..."

"No..." Chandler breathed as he increased the pace...

"Chandler... I need to go..."

"Okay... just let me get a little more... ugghhh... shit... I don't wanna stop..."

"Chandler…"

"Okay… okay…" Chandler breathed as he slowed down… "But I'ma make you pay…"

"You promise?" Starr laughed as she jumped up and hurried to the bathroom. Chandler tapped his hand impatiently on his leg as he waited for Starr to flush the toilet… "Okay… that's better…" she said as she came out the bathroom, got back in bed, and started stroking Chandler's dick…

"Uh uh…" he said as he took her hand off him…

"Chandler!"

"What?"

"Don't you want me?"

"Always…" he said as he kissed her…

"So why can't I touch you then?"

"You can…" Chandler breathed as he pushed Starr onto her back and eased himself inside her…

"Ooohhh… this is what you want…" she breathed…

"Yes…" Chandler breathed… "This… is… what… I… want… ugghh…"

"Oooohhh… Chandler…"

"Yes… Starr…"

"Give it to me…"

"Okay…" Chandler breathed as he picked up the pace…

"Oooohhh… Oooohhh… Oooohhh…"

"Is this what you want?"

"Yes Chandler... Yes... Oooohhh..."

"Tell me again..."

"Give it to me... please..."

"Yeeesss..." Chandler breathed as he picked up Starr's legs and thrust deeper...

"Oh Chandler... Yes... Like that..."

"Like that?"

"Yes... Oh God..."

"Mmmm... your pussy's so wet... you love this dick... don't you?"

"Yes Chandler... give it to me... I love it..."

"Uggh! Uggh! Uggh! Uggh! Uggh!"

"Chandler... Yes... Yes... "Oooohhh... Oooohhh... Oooohhh... Ooooooohhhhhh!"

"Yes... that's it... I love it when you come all over my dick... Fuck... Uuuggghhhh!" Chandler didn't move and Starr didn't want him to...

"Do we have to get up now?"

"Yes..."

"Why?"

"So we can meet your parents at breakfast... and surprise them..."

"Okay... I'll get up..."

"Okay..." Chandler breathed...

"Chandler..." Starr laughed...

"What?"

"I can't get up – until you get up..."

"Okay..." Chandler said as he got up... "C'mon – come take a shower with me..."

Chandler said as he pulled her by the hand towards the shower..."

"Okay..." she laughed... "I'm coming..." When they got in the shower Chandler turned on the shower and pushed Starr up against the wall...

"Chandler... we can't..." We'll make it quick..." he said as he sat on the bench and spread Starr's legs... "Chandler... huh... huh..." Chandler took her clit in his mouth and sucked hard... "Chandler... I'm gonna cum... Huh... Huh... Huh... Huh... Huuuggghhh!" Chandler pushed Starr towards his mouth and continued sucking until she stopped him... "Chandler... it's sensitive..."

"I love you..." Chandler said as he held her and looked up at her..."

"Get up..." Starr commanded...

"Yes Maam..." Chandler laughed as he stood up. Starr sat down on the bench and grabbed Chandler's ass...

"Watch me..." Starr commanded as she took Chandler's dick in her mouth...

"Starr... Fuck..."

"You like this?" she breathed...

"Hell yea..."

"So..." she said in between sucks... "Which do you prefer... this..." she said as she grabbed his dick with her hand and sucked the head... "Or this..." she said as she grabbed his ass and pushed his dick all the way into her mouth down to his balls...

"Starr... Fuck!"

"Which do you prefer?"

"Just pick one... or both... I don't care!"

"Hmmmm... you said one... or both... I'll do neither..." she said as she started jerking his dick...

"Starr... oh shit... uggh!"

"You like that too?"

"Hell yea!"

"Aww..." she said as she took his dick in her mouth and sucked a little... "Now I don't know what to do..." she sighed playfully as she stroked his dick...

"Starr... please..." Chandler breathed...

"Ooohhh..." she said as she put her mouth on his dick and sucked a little more... "Did you say please?"

"Yes... please..." he breathed...

"Okay... since you said please..." she said and then she took Chandler's dick in her mouth and sucked it...

"Starr... oh shit... Starr..." Chandler moaned as he grabbed her head with his hands and let her suck his dick at her pace... "Starr... suck it... yes... shit..." Starr could feel Chandler's body tensing up so she quickened her pace... "Starr... Ooohhh... Ooohhh... Ooohhh... Uuuuggghhhh! Fuck!" Starr swallowed and continued sucking until Chandler stopped shaking...

"Are we done now?" she asked as she stood up and Chandler pulled her to him and held her...

"Hell no..." Chandler breathed as he kissed her...

"Chandler!"

"We gon' take a shower – we gon' get dressed – we gon' go have breakfast – we gon' see your parents – but we ain't never – ever – gon' be done – you understand me?"

"Yes Chandler..." she said as she kissed him... "I understand you..."

"That's better – now let's take a shower, get dressed, and get outta here...

"Mary..." Wayne whispered...

"Yes Wayne?" I answered sleepily...

"We need to get up..."

"Do we have to?"

"No... we can stay in bed if you want..."

"I'll get up – I know you're trying to save money..." I said as I got up...

"We can come back to bed if you want..."

"I might take you up on that..." I said as I went into the bathroom and turned on the shower...

"May I join you?"

"Always..." I answered...

"I love you Mary..." Wayne said as he pulled me into a kiss...

"I love you too..."

"Can I have some? Please?"

"Wayne..."

"Please... you're not gonna leave me like this?" he said as he took my hand and put it on his dick...

"Oh my..." I breathed... "I guess I can do something... what would you like?"

"I want everything..."

"Everything?"

"Everything..."

"What time is it?"

"A lil' after 7..."

"Okay... c'mere..." I said as I took his dick in my mouth...

"Yes Mommy... suck it..." I was tired but I loved pleasing Wayne. I loved hearing him call me Mommy when he moaned... and it was making me wet... and he knew it...

"Mommy... let me taste your pussy..." I was sopping wet as soon as I stood up, anticipating what Wayne was gonna do... and then he surprised me... "Turn around... brace yourself..."

"Yes Daddy..." I breathed. I thought Wayne was gonna fuck me from behind when he grabbed my waist but he didn't... "Wayne!" I moaned as he spread my cheeks and stuck his tongue in my ass...

"Mmmm... Mmmm..." Wayne moaned. Wayne sucked my ass good as he began playing with my pussy and I was in heaven... "You like that Mommy?"

"Yes Daddy! Yes!" I moaned as Wayne's tongue danced inside my ass and up the crack of my ass as he played with my pussy... "Huh... Huh... Huh... Huh..."

"You ready for Daddy?"

"Yes Daddy... I'm ready..." I breathed. Wayne stood up, spread my cheeks, eased himself inside, and began fucking my ass as he played with my clit... "Yes Daddy! Yes!" Fuck my ass!" Wayne grabbed me by my waist with both hands and fucked me harder as I played with my pussy...

"You like this Mommy?"

"Yes Daddy! I love it! Haahh!" Wayne was hitting my G-spot and I was playing with my clit so I was throbbing inside and out... "Daddy you gon' make me cum..." I moaned...

"Not yet Mommy... hold it..." Wayne said as he pulled out my ass, turned me around, put my leg up on the bench and thrust himself inside me...

"Oh God! Yes! Fuck me!"

"You ready Mommy?"

"Yes Daddy! Yes! Fuck me!" Wayne held me and continued fucking me as he took my breast in his mouth and sucked it... "Ooohhh... Ooohhh... That's it... right there... right there...

yes... don't stop... don't stop... I'm cumming! Aaahhhhh! Aaahhhhh! Aaahhhhh! Aaahhhhh!" I collapsed as Wayne held me up...

"I gotchu Mommy..." Wayne breathed as he kissed me...

"Wayne... I don't know what's gotten into me..." I breathed...

"That would be me..." Wayne laughed...

"I guess you're right..." I laughed...

"You ready for Daddy?"

"Yes Daddy..." I breathed... "I'm ready..."

"How you want it?"

"Anyway you wanna give it to me..." I breathed...

"Hmmm... shall I give it to you here?" he asked as he kissed me... "Or here?" he said as he pushed his dick up inside me...

"Ooohhh..." I moaned...

"Or..." he said as he pulled out, turned me around, bent me over, and thrust himself in my ass... "Here?"

"There..." I breathed...

"Okay Mommy..." he breathed as he grabbed my waist and started fucking my ass...

"Oh yes... fuck me..." I moaned. Every time Wayne fucked me in my pussy 'till I came, I'd always come again when he fucked my ass... and today was no exception... "Yes Daddy... Yes..."

"Ugghh... Ugghh... Ugghh..."

"Fuck me... fuck me... fuck me..."

"Uggh! Uggh! Uggh! Uggh!"

"I'm cumming Daddy... I'm cumming..."

"Come for Daddy Mommy..."

"Aaagh! Aaagh! Aaagh! Aaagh!"

"Uggh! Uggh! Uggh! Uggh! Uuuggghhhh! Mommy... what the fuck are you doing to me?" he breathed in my ear as he laid on my back and held me...

"Same thing you're doing to me..." I breathed as he massaged my breasts...

"Mmmm... your pussy's still wet..." he breathed as he played with my clit...

"Ooohhh... Wayne..."

"Yes... stand up..." I stood up, he sat on the bench in front of me... spread my legs... and flicked his tongue on my clit...

"Oooohhh... Oooohhh... Oooohhh..." Wayne pushed me to his face, grabbed my ass, and sucked... "Aaahh... Wayne... Aaahh..."

"Mmmph... Mmmph... Mmmph... Mmmph..."

"Hmmm... Hmmm.... Hmmm... Hmmm..."

"Mmmph... Mmmph... Mmmph... Mmmph..."

"I'm cummin... I'm cummin... Huh... Huh... Huh..."

"Mmmph... Mmmph... Mmmph... Mmmph..." Wayne continued sucking and slurping after my legs shook and I had to stop him...

"Wayne... stop..."

"You sure?"

"Yes..." I breathed... "I'm sure..."

"Okay..." he breathed... "I'll stop... for now..."

"Good – now let's get a shower, get dressed, and get downstairs to breakfast before I change my mind..." I laughed...

Chapter 2

"They have good food... and great coffee..." Starr said...

"They do..." Chandler agreed...

"I wanna stay here next time..."

"We can..." Chandler said...

"I can't wait to get breakfast – we really worked up an appetite..." I said as we walked into the dining room... and my heart sank...

"Mommy!" Starr squealed when she saw me...

"Hey Starr... Chandler..." I smiled...

"Hello Starr..." Wayne said...

"Hi Wayne – sorry..." she laughed...

"Hello Mary, Hello Wayne – sit – have breakfast with us..." Chandler said...

" Mary – you sit – I'll get us some coffee..." Wayne said as he went to get coffee...

"So... this is a surprise..." I said...

"Mommy – I was so scared when you said there was a fire..." Starr said as Wayne came back to the table with coffee...

"We're okay Starr..." Wayne said...

"That's why I'm here…" Chandler said…

"I don't understand…" Wayne said…

"I'm here to make sure you're okay…"

"Thank you Chandler – but that isn't necessary…"

"Yes it is…" Starr said…

"Starr – you were worried? About me?"

"Of course…"

"Thank you Starr…"

"I never said I didn't care about you…" she laughed…

"So… how long are you staying?" I asked…

"'Till Sunday…"

"Sunday? Oh wow – so you're going home on Sunday?"

"Depends on what happens with you…" Chandler said…

"Huh?"

"I wanna make sure you're okay before we leave…"

"You don't have to do that Chandler – Wayne's taking great care of me…"

"Let me get us some breakfast…" Wayne said as he got up…

"Well I'ma hang around – just in case…"

"That's very nice of you…"

"Mary – I told you – you're important to Starr – that means you're important to me…"

"Well I think Starr's lucky to have such a good, caring husband…" Wayne said as he sat down with our food and I started eating…

"Thank you Wayne..." Starr said...

"So what'd the insurance company say?" Chandler asked...

"Let's not talk about that now – I'm still sleepy - in fact – I'm thinking about going back to bed after breakfast..." I said...

"Wow Mommy – you must be really tired..." Starr said

"I am honey – it's been a lot..."

"Yes – I bet..." Chandler said...

"Well – we're in room 315 – what room are you in Mommy?"

"I'll call you later..." I said as I got up... "Have a nice day – and thanks for coming to check up on me – give me a hug..."

"Okay Mommy – I love you..." she said as she hugged me...

"Thank you Chandler..." I said as I hugged him...

"You're welcome Mary..." Chandler said...

"We'll call you later Chandler..." Wayne said...

"Bye Wayne – see ya later..." Starr said as we left the dining room. I didn't say anything until we got in the room and Wayne closed the door...

"Mary – what's wrong?"

"I know Chandler means well – but I was starting to feel like we were on our honeymoon..." I sighed...

"I understand..."

"I want to be free and uninhibited – I can't do that with Starr around..."

"Yes you can..."

"No I can't – she wants to know what room we're staying in – all I need is for her to interrupt us fucking!"

"Mary... calm down..." Wayne said as he pulled me into a hug...

"Chandler's up to something..."

"What makes you say that?"

"He already talked to us on the phone – why is he here?"

"Mary – you're making too much outta this... calm down..."

"No I'm not – why is he asking us about what the insurance company had to say?"

"Mary... he's just concerned... please... calm down..."

"I can't shake this feeling – Chandler's up to something – I know it..."

"You wanna lie back down?"

"Yea..."

"Okay..."

"C'mon..." Wayne said as he took me towards the bed... "Come lay down... with me..."

"Okay..." I sighed.

"Mommy's mad at me..."

"No she isn't..."

"Yes she is – she didn't even want to talk to me..." Starr said as she started tearing up...

"Starr?"

"Yes Chandler?"

"Stop it..."

"But Chandler..."

"Stop it..."

"But I..."

"I said..." and then he kissed her... "Stop it... okay?"

"Okay... I'll stop..."

"Your mother's been through a lot..."

"I know..."

"We're going to go back to our room... relax... and later tonight... we'll go to dinner..."

"Okay..." Starr said as they got up from the table and went to the elevator. When they got to their room, Chandler opened the door and Starr went straight to bed...

"Tired huh?"

"Kinda..."

"Me too..." Chandler said as he snuggled in beside her. Chandler turned on the television and watched the news until Starr fell asleep, and then he got outta bed, went to the table, and made a call from his cell...

"This is Jeremy..."

"Hey Jeremy – its Chandler..."

"Hey! How's married life?"

"Wonderful…"

"Aww… that's great – my mother talks about your wife all the time…"

"She's pregnant…"

"Congratulations!"

"Thank you…"

"Now that we've done the small talk – what's going on?"

"How'd you know?"

"You called my cell…"

"I need a favor…"

"Oh boy…"

"My wife's parents – their home was destroyed…"

"Sorry to hear that – how are they?"

"They're okay – but they're homeless…"

"Aww man…"

"The insurance is covering their hotel and they'll be issued a check after the adjusters finish their investigation…"

"Chandler?"

"Yea?"

"What aren't' you telling me?"

"Wayne Robinson…"

"That name sounds familiar…"

"He's married to Mary Smith Robinson…"

"I'll look into it – and I'll get back to you…"

"Thank you Jeremy…"

Wayne looked down at Mary sleeping peacefully and smiled... "Good – now I can get on my laptop..." he said as he opened his laptop, logged on to realtor.com, and started searching... "Oh wow..." he said out loud as he clicked on a 3-bedroom, 2-bath home in the Country Meadows Mobile Home Community... "I need to have the agent get back to me asap..." he said out loud as he filled out the form letting them know he was interested... "Master bath, pool, game room, playground, basketball court, gym, laundry, close to shopping, central heat and air... Vanessa Garcia..."

"Wayne?" I yawned...

"Yes Mary?"

"What are you doing over there?"

"Come sit with me – let me show you..."

"Okay..." I said as I got up and came to sit with Wayne..."

"Oh wow..."

"It's beautiful – isn't it?"

"Yes! It offers so much more – and it's 3 bedrooms and 2 bathrooms!"

"Starr and Chandler can come visit with the baby..."

"Oh Wayne – can we go see it?" Please?"

"Yes..."

"When?"

"I'm waiting for Vanessa Garcia to call me back..."

"I hope she calls you back today..." I said as Wayne's phone rang...

"Good morning..."

"May I speak with Wayne Robinson?"

"This is Wayne..."

"Hi Wayne – this is Vanessa Garcia – I'm calling in response to your interest in 1855 Riverside Drive..."

"Hello Vanessa – thank you for getting back to me so quickly..."

"You're welcome – I have some time now if you'd like to see it..."

"I'd like that..."

"Okay – do you need me to pick you up?"

"Yes – thank you..."

"Okay – what's your address?"

"Right now were staying at the Azure Hotel & Suites..."

"You're staying at a hotel?"

'Yes..."

"Oh so you need a place to stay asap!"

"Yes..."

"Okay – it's about 11 a.m. – I can come get you at 12 – how's that sound?"

"That sounds great..."

"Great! I'll see you then – oh one more thing – are you working with a realtor?"

"No..."

"Okay – I'll see you at 12..."

"What'd she say?"

"She'll be here at 12 to take us to see the property..."

"Oh Wayne – I love you so much!" I said as I started kissing Wayne all over his face...

"Oh yea? How much?" Wayne asked as he picked me up, carried me to the bed, laid me down, and laid on top of me...

"This much..." I said as I kissed him...

"That's not enough..." he said as he unbuttoned my blouse and massaged my breasts...

"Oh Wayne..."

"How much do you love me?"

"This much..." I moaned...

"That's still not enough..." he said as he unzipped my pants and slid them down...

"How much do you love me?"

"Oh Wayne... this much..."

"Still not enough..." he said as he unzipped his pants, took out his dick, and eased himself inside me...

"Wayne... oh Wayne..."

"How much do you love me?"

"This much... huh..."

"Still not enough..." he breathed in my ear as I grabbed his ass and pushed him in deeper...

"Wayne... Wayne... Wayne..." I moaned as I spread my legs wider...

"Yes... that's more like it..." Wayne breathed as he held me underneath my back and fucked me harder...

"Wayne... Wayne... Wayne..."

"Yes Mary... Yes..."

"Don't stop... Don't stop..."

"How much do you love me?" he growled as he thrust in deeper...

"Oh God... this much..."

"Like this?"

"Yes Wayne... Yes..."

"Show me..."

"Wayne... Yes... Yes..." I moaned as I dug my nails in his back...

"How much do you love me Mary?"

"Fuck me... I'm cumming... I'm cumming..."

"Yes... Mary... show me how much you love me..."

"Aaagh! Aaagh! Aaagh! Aaagh! Aaaaagggghhhhh!"

"Yes..." Wayne breathed as he kissed me... "Now... I'm gonna fuck you... and show you... how much... I... love... you..." he breathed as he picked up my legs, bent them in the knees, and fucked me harder...

"Wayne! Oh God... Oh God..."

"Uuugh! Uuugh! Uuugh! Uuugh! Uuuugggghhhh!" Wayne collapsed in me and stayed inside me, kissing me...

"Hhhmph... Hhhmph... Hhhmph... Hhhmph..."

"Mmmph... Mmmph... Mmmph... Mmmph..."

"What time is it?" I breathed...

"It's 11:22..."

"Shit..."

"What's wrong?"

"We need to get ready..."

"We can do that..."

"But I want some more..."

"Let me see what I can do..." Wayne breathed as he picked up my legs, bent them at the knee, and started fucking me again...

"Ooohhh... Ooohhhh... Ooohhhh..."

"This is Chandler..."

"It's Jeremy..."

"What'd you find out?"

"They both worked for Bazil Osgood..."

"Both?"

"Yes..."

"What happened?"

"Remember when I told you his name sounded familiar?"

"Yea..."

"They were both charged with embezzling over $50,000 from Osgood Publishing..."

"Both of them were charged?"

"Yea – but Mary took the rap..."

"What happened to Wayne?"

"Wayne disappeared after Mary went to jail...

"Did they ever make restitution?"

"According to our records... no..."

"This is starting to make sense…"

"What's starting to make sense?"

"Wayne and Mary were together for 18 years – Wayne thought my wife was his daughter…"

"I don't understand…"

"Wayne left when my wife was 18… her mother went to jail…"

"I still don't understand…"

"They got married on Monday… they came here Friday… their house was burned down…"

"Chandler – what are you saying?"

"They never made restitution…"

"I still don't get it…"

"Where'd the money come from to buy their home?"

"Oh shit!"

"Now you understand…"

"Chandler… are you telling me…."

"I'm not telling you anything… but I need you to check something else for me…"

"Watcha need?"

"Jermoll made Mary the beneficiary on his pension…"

"What?"

"Long story – anyway – find out what her monthly benefit is – and get back to me…"

"You got it…"

"Chandler?"

"Yes Starr?"

"Who were you talking to?"

"Work…"

"How long was I asleep?"

"About an hour…"

"Let's go out…"

"You wanna go out?"

"Yea…"

"Okay – c'mon – let's go…" Chandler said as Starr got up and they went downstairs…

"I'm so excited – I can't wait for Vanessa to get here…" I said as I held Wayne's hand…

"Who's Vanessa?" Starr asked…

"Oh hey Starr… Chandler…"

"Hey – y'all on your way out?" Chandler asked…

"Yes…" Wayne answered…

"Mind if we tag along?" Chandler asked…

"Mary?" Wayne asked as he held me and looked at me…

"I guess if Vanessa has room…" I laughed as Vanessa pulled up…

"Good afternoon – are you Wayne Robinson?"

"I'm Wayne – this is my wife Mary, our daughter Starr, and her husband Chandler…"

"Oh nice… now I see why you need three bedrooms – come on in – I have room – I just need someone to sit in the front…"

"I'll sit in the front…" Wayne said as he opened the door for us to get in and then he got in. Chandler went to get in and sat behind Vanessa...

"I'm so glad you reached out to me – this unit's only been on the market for 16 days – the owner will be happy..."

"You have other units?" Wayne asked...

"Yes..."

"When was this home built?"

"1970..."

"Okay... we're here..." Vanessa said as she parked the car...

"Hmmm – Country Meadows Mobile Home Park..." Chandler said...

"This looks nice Mommy..." Starr said...

"It is – it's actually nicer than the one we had..." I said as we started walking...

"You had a mobile home before? Where?" Vanessa asked...

"Here..." Wayne answered...

"Will this be your second home?"

"No – it'll be our first..." Wayne answered... "The home we had was in a fire..."

"Oh my goodness – was anyone hurt?"

"No..."

"Thank God..."

"You're welcome..." God said...

"Here it is..." Vanessa said as we walked up to it...

"Why is the door on the side?" Starr asked...

"The other side as the car port..." Vanessa answered...

"What's a car port?"

"It's for parking – wanna see?"

"Okay..." Starr said as we waked around to the car port...

"Hmmm... nice size..." Chandler said...

"It's big enough for two cars..." Vanessa said...

"Let's go inside!" I said...

"Sure – c'mon..." Vanessa said as she opened the door and we walked inside...

"I like it already..." I said...

"Well that's nice..." Vanessa said as Chandler and Starr looked around...

"I like to too..." Wayne said...

"Mommy – this is a big kitchen..." Starr said...

"Yes it is – and I have room for a dining room table..."

"Sounds like you see yourself living here..." Vanessa said...

"I do..." Wayne and Vanessa smiled, but Chandler stayed quiet...

"Mommy – you have a master bedroom!"

"I know..." I said as I looked at Wayne and smiled...

"Hmmm – 3 bedrooms – nice size – guest room – office..." Chandler said...

"We were thinking guest room... nursery..." Wayne said...

"You're pregnant? Congratulations!" Vanessa said...

"Thank you..." I laughed... "But I'm not pregnant – she is..." I said as I pulled Starr into a hug...

"Aww... Congratulations..." Vanessa said...

"Thank you..." Starr said...

"Well – now that you've seen everything – let me show you the amenities..." Vanessa said...

"Okay..." I said as we followed Vanessa outside...

"The unit has heat and central air and inside laundry..."

"Oh that's music to my ears!" I said...

"As you can see, the association has two pools – there's also a game room, two club houses, a playground, basketball courts, and a gym..."

"Very nice!" Wayne said as we continued walking around...

"What's the crime rate here?" Chandler asked...

"Well – I'm not going to tell you crime doesn't happen – but what I can tell you is this is one of the better neighborhoods..." Vanessa answered. To be honest – it didn't matter how she answered – I'd already made up my mind this would be our new home... "Okay – if you don't have any questions, I'll take you back to the hotel..." Vanessa said...

"I don't have any questions..." I sighed. Wayne took my hand and we walked hand-in-hand to Vanessa's car and got in...

"So – not to be pushy – but can I expect an offer?" she laughed...

"Possibly..." Wayne answered...

"I'll take that..." Vanessa laughed. We rode back to the hotel without speaking. Starr was smiling but Chandler seemed to be pre-occupied... "Here we are..." Vanessa said as she pulled up in front of the hotel...

"Thank you Vanessa..." Wayne said...

"You're very welcome..."

"I'll see you upstairs – I need to talk to Vanessa..." Wayne said...

"Okay..." I sighed as I went into the hotel..."

"Mommy – wait..." Starr said as she hurried to catch up to me...

"I'll see you inside..." Chandler said to Wayne...

"Is there something you wanted to tell me?" Vanessa asked...

"My wife and I are newlyweds..."

"Congratulations!"

"We were married on Monday and came here Friday. I thought we would be starting our new life together in our new home but that didn't happen..."

"Oh my God – I' so sorry..."

"I just want to make my wife happy – if I can buy this home for us, I can keep that smile on her face..."

"You're wife's a lucky woman..."

"I'm the lucky one – we were together for 18 years – we broke up – a dear friend reached out to me in facebook and told me where Mary was – I went to see her – I asked her to marry me – she said yes..."

"Oh my God... this is such a beautiful story..." Vanessa said as she started dabbing her eyes with a tissue...

"We had homeowner's insurance – I'm just not sure if the check will be enough to cover the asking price..."

"Well – I represent the seller – but if you make an offer I'll present it and we'll see what we can do..."

"Thank you Vanessa..." Wayne said as he hugged her...

"You're welcome – please let me know..." she said as she got back in her car and drove off...

"What'd she say?" I asked as Wayne came into the lobby...

"She said she represents the seller but if we make an offer she'll present it to him..."

"I hope you get it Mommy – I like it..."

"So do I Starr..."

"Watcha doin' for the rest of the day?" Chandler asked...

"We didn't really have any plans... you?" Wayne asked...

"We didn't really have any plans either – how 'bout we relax for a couple of hours and meet back here at 5 for dinner – my treat?"

"Thank you Chandler – we'll see you at 5..."

"Okay – see you soon..."

"Mommy?"

"Yes Starr?"

"What room are you in?"

"I'll call you later..." I laughed as Wayne and I got in the elevator and went back to our room...

"Why does she keep doing that?" Starr laughed...

"I love you..." Chandler laughed...

"I love you too Chandler..."

"What are we going to do until 5 o'clock?" Chandler pulled Starr next to him and whispered in her ear...

"The same thing your parent's are doing..."

"Ooohhh..." Starr laughed as they went to the elevator and went to their room.

Chapter 3

"I need to take this..." Chandler said as soon as they got in their room and closed the door... "This is Chandler..."

"I got something for you..."

"Hold on – Starr – I'ma be a few minutes..."

"Okay Chandler..." she said as she got in the bed and turned on the television...

"Okay – tell me..."

"Can you talk?"

"I can listen..."

"Well... you're not gonna believe this..."

"What is it?"

"Mary isn't getting any money..."

"What?"

"Jermoll took out a loan against his pension for $50,000 before he died..."

"Get the fuck outta here!"

"Mary got a check for $5,000... that's it!"

"What about the $50,000?"

"Jermoll deposited that check – made a cash withdrawal for $50,000... that's it..."

"He didn't give it to Mary?"

"Mary only has $5,000 in her checking account…"

"No other activity?"

"No…"

"What the hell did he do with that money?"

"That $50,000 withdrawal was the last bit of activity on Jermoll's account…"

"What the fuck?"

"I wish I knew…"

"What about Wayne?"

"He worked for UPS up until June 21st…"

"Was he fired?"

"No… he resigned…

"Does he have any money?"

"He has a couple of thousand – his payroll was direct deposit – he used online banking to pay his bills…"

"He have any credit cards?"

"A few…"

"What was his address?"

"He lived in Fairfield – you want the exact address?"

"No… thank you Jeremy…"

"Listen – I need to ask you something…"

"Okay…"

"What's this got to do with you?"

"Hold on a minute…" Chandler said as he got up to leave…"

"Chandler – where are you going?"

"I need to check something for work – I'll be right back – I promise…" he said as he left the room and went down to the lobby… "Mary Smith and Wayne Robinson worked for Bazil Osgood…"

"Okay…"

"They embezzled $50,000 from him…"

"Okay…"

"Bazil Osgood is my father-in-law…"

"Chandler – are you telling me – Bazil J. Osgood – the man that was arrested for manslaughter by Detective Katina Jones – you're married to his daughter?"

"Yes…"

"Oh shit! You are the mutha fuckin' man!"

"Thank ya, thank ya…"

"How'd he take it?"

"He knocked the shit outta me…" Chandler laughed…

"What made him come around?"

"I told him I love her… and I asked for his blessing…"

"Aww damn…"

"We have a great relationship – and I have his respect…"

"Damn – does she have a sister?" Jeremy laughed…

"No…. but she has a brother…"

"A brother? Beautiee had a child?"

"Yea…"

"Oh wow – I need to keep in touch with you…"

"We can get up when I get back…"

"Chandler?"

"Yea?"

"I hate to ask…"

"Don't ask…"

"Okay…"

"Listen – I need to get back to my wife – I'll talk to you later…"

"Okay Chandler…" Jeremy said and then he hung up…

"There you are!" Starr exclaimed…

"I'm sorry…"

"I'm mad at you…" Chandler took off his clothes, climbed in bed with Starr, and started kissing her neck…

"I'm sorry…" he breathed as he kissed her neck…

"I'm still mad…"

"Please…" he whispered and then he kissed her in the mouth…

"Mmmm….."

"Does that mean you forgive me?" he asked as he unbuttoned her blouse…

"I don't know…" she breathed…

"Please…" he whispered as he removed her bra…"

"Mmmm…. I don't know…"

"Please… forgive… me…" he whispered as he touched her breasts…

"Mmmm… I don't know…" she moaned…

"Please…" he whispered as he unzipped her pants and pulled them down… "Forgive me..." he whispered as he kissed his way down her stomach...

"Ohhh... Chandler... I don't know..."

"Please..." Chandler whispered as he spread her legs and licked her clit... "Forgive me..."

"Chandler..." Starr moaned...

"Do you..." he said as he licked her clit again... "Forgive me?" he asked as he started flicking his tongue on her clit...

"Yes..."

"Mmmm... yes what?"

"Yes... I forgive you..."

"Mmmm...." Chandler moaned as he pulled Starr down on her back, spread her legs wider, and dove in...

"Chandler!" Starr screamed as Chandler devoured her... "Hah... Hah... Hah... Hah... Hah... Hah... Hah... Hah..." Chandler stopped, looked up at Starr, climbed up between her legs, and eased himself inside her... "Chandler... Hah... Hah..." Chandler picked up Starr's right leg, put it up on his shoulder, and fucked her deeper... "Chandler... Chandler... Chandler..."

"Ummph... Ummph... Ummph... Ummph... Ummph..."

"Chandler... I'm cumming... I'm cumming... Aaaahhhh!"

"Ummph! Ummph! Ummph! Ummph! Uuummmppphhh!" Chandler put Starr's leg down and kissed her hard...

"Damn..." Starr breathed... "I should get mad at you more often..."

"I'm wit it..." Chandler breathed...

"Oh Wayne..." I sighed as I threw my arms around his neck and kissed him...

"You love it – don't you?"

"Yes..."

"Me too..."

"Have you heard anything from Allstate yet?"

"No..." Wayne sighed...

"Wayne?"

"Yes Mommy?"

"Come here..." I said as I opened my arms. Wayne hugged me as I hugged him... "Give me your hand..." Wayne gave me his hand and I put it on my heart... "You feel that?"

"Yea..." I took my hand and put it on his heart...

"So do I..." I sighed as I put my head in his chest...

"I'm worried..."

"I know..."

"I'm glad Chandler's taking us out to dinner..."

"You are?"

"Yea..."

"I still think he's up to something..."

"He is..."

"So you believe me?"

"Absolutely…"

"What do you think he's up to?"

"Honestly?"

"Yea…"

"I think he wants to make sure you're really happy… with me…"

"Really?"

"Yea…"

"You think Chandler doesn't trust you?"

"He doesn't…"

"I'm sorry…"

"Don't be…"

"It doesn't bother you?"

"Not at all…"

"Wow…"

"All I've ever wanted is to make you happy…"

"I am happy…"

"I know you are… and Chandler will know it too… hold on… le'me answer that…" he said as he answered his phone… "Good afternoon…"

"Mr. Robinson?"

"This is Mr. Robinson…"

"This is Lonnie from Allstate…"

"Hello Lonnie…"

"I have an update on your claim…"

"Okay…"

"We've done an appraisal on your property and we compared it to comps in the area – and based on what you paid and our allowance for furnishings – we've reached an estimate of $48,000 – how does that sound?"

"That's sounds great…" Wayne answered…

"We'll get the check right out to you – you should get it no later than Friday…"

"We're still in the hotel – we haven't found a place yet…"

"That's kay – your policy covers you up to 30 days in a hotel – we can always extend that…"

"Thank you Lonnie…" Wayne said as he hung up…

"Wayne… what's wrong?"

"That was Lonnie from Allstate…"

"Okay…"

"We're getting $48,000…"

"That's great! Why aren't you happy?"

"Because… the asking price is $55,000…" Wayne sighed…

"Oh…"

"I'm sorry…"

"Wayne?"

"Yes Mary?"

"Make the offer…"

"We don't have $55,000…"

"Wayne…" I said as I took his hand… "Make the offer…"

"What if they don't accept it?"

"Then we'll keep looking…"

"Are you sure?"

"Yes Wayne… I'm sure…"

"Okay…" Wayne said as he called Vanessa…"

"This is Vanessa Garcia – how may I help you?"

"This is Wayne Robinson…"

"Wayne! How are you?"

"We'd like to submit an offer…"

"Wonderful! What's the amount of your offer?"

"$48,000…"

"I see… well… I'll send over the contract – sign it, and I'll present it to the seller – do you have an email?"

"Yes – it's WayneRobinson12@gmail.com…"

"Okay – I'll get it out to you right away – oh – I also need your pre-approval…"

"I don't have a pre-approval…"

"Oh… I see – well – I'll get to work on this contract and you'll have it within the hour – I'll set the closing date for two weeks from Friday…"

"Can you make it one week from Friday?"

"Wayne – we can't do that unless you're making a cash offer…"

"I'm making a cash offer…"

"Oh my goodness – that's wonderful! Let me get this contract over to you…"

"Thank you Vanessa…"

"You're welcome – and thank you…"

"Now we wait…" he said as he hung up…

"Okay…" I sighed…

"Don't say anything…"

"Why?"

"I don't wanna get Starr's hopes up... or Chandlers...

"Okay..."

"C'mon – let's go downstairs – I wanna check my email..." Wayne said as he took my hand and we went downstairs. When we got to the business center Wayne turned on the computer, logged into his email, and started deleting junk mail and spam. After entering Publisher's Clearing House, he clicked on a message from UPS and read the following attachment:

Friday, June 25, 2019

Wayne Robinson
201 East Arrow Highway
Toronto, Ontario M1E4Y1

Dear Mr.Robinson,

We are pleased to offer a full-time position at United Parcel Service with a start date of Monday, July 15th at 2900 Steeles Avenue West, L4K352 (Jane & Steeles). We are located right beside Pioneer Village subway Station.

Because you have prior experience with UPS, your hourly rate will be $18.00 per hour with an automatic progression up to $30.00 per hour, paid on a weekly basis by direct deposit, starting on July 25th.

As an employee of UPS, you are also eligible for our benefits program, which includes the following:

. Health and dental benefits after one year
. 2 weeks paid vacation after one year
. Employee Referral Bonus Program
. Access to UPS employee Discounts
. Paid training
. Opportunity for advancement
. Free parking

Please confirm your acceptance of this offer by signing and returning this letter by July 5th, 2019.

We are excited to have you join our team! If you have any questions, please feel free to reach out at any time.

Sincerely,

Jane Steele
UPS District Coordinator
1-800-742-5877

"Mary..." Wayne whispered...

"Yes Wayne?"

"Look..." he whispered as he pointed to the letter and I read it...

"Oh Wayne... congratulations..." I said as he pulled me into a kiss...

"Oh my God... I can't believe it..."

"Why not?"

"When I asked them if I could transfer they told me I couldn't because I was leaving the country... they said I'd have to apply as a new employee and start over..."

"When did you apply for this job?"

"I applied before I asked you to marry me..."

"You applied in Connecticut?"

"I was working for UPS in Fairfield – I told them I was moving to Canada and they told me I couldn't transfer – so I resigned..."

"You had this planned from the beginning?"

"Kinda..."

"Kinda?"

"I wasn't sure you'd say yes..."

"I'm glad I did..."

"So am I..." Wayne breathed as he kissed me...

"Oh – here's the email from Vanessa..." Wayne said as he pulled up the contract and read it... "I'm going to print out this letter and this contract – I'll sign the letter and scan it back to

UPS – then we'll sign the contract and get the offer over to Vanessa…"

"We?"

"Yes Mary…"

"Okay…" I sighed. Wayne printed out the letter, signed it, and scanned it back to his email and then he printed out the contract…

"Okay Mrs. Robinson – I need you to initial here – where I added your name…"

"Okay…" I sighed as he handed me the pen, I initialed, and gave the pen back to him…

"Okay – now…" he said as he kissed me… "I need your signature…"

"Okay…" I sighed as he handed me the pen again, I signed the contract, and handed him back the pen…"

"Okay – let's get this back over to Vanessa…" he said as I watched him scan it back to his email, attach it, and hit send…."

"I'm so excited – let's go back upstairs…" I said…

"Don't you wanna wait to see if they accept our offer?"

"No…."

"Okay – let's go back upstairs then…" Wayne said as I got up, he logged off the computer, took my hand, and we went back to our room. As soon as the door was closed Wayne pushed me back against the door and started kissing me…

"Wayne… what time is it?" I breathed…

"Ssshhhh..." Wayne whispered as he led me to the bed, pushed me down, laid on top of me, and started kissing me again...

"Wayne..." I moaned. Wayne ran his hands over my breasts and down my body and then he lifted my shirt and began sucking and squeezing on my breasts... "Wayne... I moaned as I grabbed his head and pushed him down my body. Wayne kissed his way down my stomach, opened my pants... and then the phone rang...

"Who the hell is that?" Wayne snapped...

"Who else?" I laughed...

"Starr?"

"Answer the phone Wayne..." I laughed...

"Good afternoon..."

"Hi... Dad..."

"Hi Starr..." I saw tears in Wayne's eyes and I got concerned...

"Can I speak to Mommy?"

"Sure..."Wayne said as he handed me the phone...

"Yes Starr?"

"Hi Mommy..."

"Hi Starr..."

"Chandler made reservations for us at Carisma at 5:30..."

"Okay..."

"It's an Italian restaurant..."

"Sounds good..."

"I'll see you later..."

"Okay Starr..." I said as I hung up the phone and sat up on the bed next to Wayne... "What's wrong?"

"She called me Dad..."

"Aww..."

"Dammit – what now?" Wayne said as he answered his cell... "Good afternoon..."

"Wayne – this is Vanessa..."

"Hello Vanessa..."

"I have something I need to tell you..."

"Okay..." Wayne sighed as he put his hand on his head...

"We received another offer on the property..."

"Okay..."

"I presented both offers to the seller..."

"Okay..."

"And the seller couldn't really decide which offer to take... so..."

"Yes Vanessa?"

"Well... I shouldn't be telling you this..."

"Okay..."

"If anyone ever finds out..."

"I won't tell anyone but my wife..."

"Well... okay – I'm just going to say it..."

"Okay..."

"I told the seller I met your family and I told the seller how you found love again after all this time..."

"Aww... that's okay..."

"He's very happy for you and your wife..."

"Aww... that's very sweet..."

"He's so happy for you that he decided to accept your offer..."

"Vanessa! Why would you do that?" Wayne laughed...

"I'm sorry..." she laughed...

"So what happens now?"

"Well – until we get the check – I can't tell you it's officially yours – so it will still be listed – but it will say contingent – that means its contingent on everything going through..."

"Okay - I'll keep you posted – thank you Vanessa..."

"You're welcome – have a great evening – and congratulations..."

"Thank you Vanessa..."

"What happened?" I asked...

"Another offer came in on the property..."

"Aww... that's okay – we'll get the next one..."

"Mary?"

"Yes Wayne?"

"Vanessa presented both offers..."

"Okay..."

"Vanessa told the seller about how we found love again..."

"Aww..."

"He was so happy for us he decided to accept our offer..."

"We got it?"

"As long as the check clears... we got it..."

"Oh my God! We got it!" I squealed as I jumped up off the bed. Wayne stood up, took me in his arms, kissed me hard, pushed me back down on the bed, took down my pants, and growled...

"I don't give a damn who calls – I'm not answering the phone or the door until I get some pussy..." and then he spread my legs and eased himself inside me...

"Wayne..." I moaned and it was all I could get out because Wayne pushed me back, put his tongue in my mouth, covered my mouth with his, and tongued me down as he wrapped his arm under my back, held me, and fucked me...

"Mmmph! Mmmph! Mmmph! Mmmph!"
"Hmmph! Hmmph! Hmmph! Hmmph!"
"Mmmph! Mmmph! Mmmph! Mmmph!"
"Hmmph! Hmmph! Hmmph! Hmmph!" I opened my legs wider and Wayne lifted my ass up off the bed and fucked me harder as he continued tonguing me down...

"Mmmph! Mmmph! Mmmph! Mmmph!"
"Hmmph! Hmmph! Hmmph! Hmmph!"
"Mmmph! Mmmph! Mmmph! Mmmph!"
"Hmmph! Hmmph! Hmmph! Hmmph!" I picked up my legs and locked my ankles around Wayne's back as my legs shook...

"Mmmph! Mmmph! Mmmph! Mmmph!"
"Hmmph! Hmmph! Hmmph! Hmmph!"
"Mmmph! Mmmph! Mmmph! Mmmph!"

"Hmmph! Hmmph! Hmmph! Hmmph!" I grabbed Wayne's ass and pushed him in deeper as my orgasm ran up my body... "Mmmph! Mmmph! Mmmph! Mmmph!"

"Hmmph! Hmmph! Hmmph! Hmmph!"

"Mmmph! Mmmph! Mmmph! Mmmph!"

"Hmmph! Hmmph! Hmmph! Hmmph!" Wayne and I continued holding and kissing each other as our orgasms subsided...

"Mommy..." Wayne breathed...

"Yes Daddy... Yes..." I breathed... and then the phone rang...

"Yes Starr?" Wayne answered...

"Are you on your way downstairs?"

"What time is it?"

"It's 5 o'clock..."

"Okay – we're on our way..." Wayne said as we jumped up outta bed, threw our clothes on, and hurried downstairs.

Chapter 4

"There you are!" Starr exclaimed...

"Here we are..." I said...

"They have Ubers here?" Chandler asked...

"I think so..." Wayne answered...

"Okay – I'll order one..." Chandler said as he took out his phone...

"Where's Carisma?" Wayne asked...

"It's right downtown..." Chandler answered...

"Thank you Chandler..." I said...

"You're welcome Mary..."

"C'mon – the Uber's here!" Starr squealed as she went outside...

"She's certainly excited..." Wayne said...

"Yea – you know how she gets when she's happy..." I said as we went outside to get in the Uber. Wayne got in the front and I got in the back with Starr and Chandler. We looked out the window as the uber driver took us downtown...

"Oh look – there it is!" Starr exclaimed...

"Hmmm – they have a lot of restaurants down here – we'll have to try them all..." Wayne said...

"We can do that..." Chandler said as we went inside...

"Oh Chandler – this is nice..." I said...

"It is, it is..." Chandler agreed...

"Do you have a reservation?" the owner asked...

"Corbett..." Chandler answered...

"Right this way..." he said as we followed him to the table and sat down... "Your server will be right with you..." the owner said as he walked away...

"So... let's celebrate..." Chandler said...

"What are we celebrating?"

"Today is Tuesday..." Chandler said...

"Okay..." Wayne said...

"Y'all got married Monday..."

"Oh wow..." I said...

"Happy One Week Anniversary..." Wayne said as he kissed me...

"Happy One Week Anniversary..." I sighed as I kissed him back...

"Aww... Happy Anniversary..." Starr said...

"Thank you Starr, thank you Chandler..." Wayne said...

"It's been a tough week I bet..." Chandler said...

"It's been challenging... but we'll be okay..." Wayne said as he took my hand and kissed it...

"May I start you off with something to drink?" the waiter asked...

"I'll have a ginger ale..." Starr said...

"I'll have a Pear Te..." Chandler said...

"I'll have a Pear Te too..." Wayne said...

"I'll have a Pear Te as well..." I said...

"What's a Pear Te?" Starr asked...

"It's alcohol honey..." I answered...

"Can I taste it?"

"Sure..."

"I'll be back with your drinks..." the waiter said as he went to place our order...

"Does anyone want caviar?" Chandler asked...

"No..." Wayne answered...

"What's caviar?" Starr asked...

"Fish eggs..." Chandler answered...

"Eww!"

"Try it..." Chandler said...

"Chandler... I don't want to eat a fish egg..."

"Try it..."

"What if I don't like it?"

"Then don't eat it..."

"Okay... I'll try it..." she sighed...

"It's not bad Starr... it's just not for me..." I said...

"I eat it..." Wayne said as he turned to look at me and smiled...

"Dad!" Starr exclaimed as we laughed at her...

"What'd I say?" Wayne asked innocently...

"Anyway..." Chandler interrupted... "They have grilled calamari..."

"I normally eat that fried..." I said...

"What's calamari?" Starr asked...

"Octopus..." I answered...

"Oh no – I definitely don't want that!"

"I never wanted it either – until I tried it..." I said...

"Is it good Mommy?"

"I like it..."

"Try it..." Chandler said...

"Okay..." Starr sighed...

"Here's your drinks – the waiter said as he placed the drinks on the table...

"May I take your order for appetizers or a salad?"

"We'll have the Calamari alla Griglia, the Carpaccio Di Manzo, the Caesante Con Foi Gras, and the Cozze Al Guazzetto... and we'll have some caviar..." Chandler answered...

"Russe or Classic Ossetra?"

"Classic Ossetra..."

"Okay... I'll be right back..."

"Chandler?"

"Yes Wayne?"

"What did you just order?"

"I ordered calamari, beef tenderloin, scallops, and mussels..."

"Wow – I'm impressed – how'd you know all that?"

"I read the menu..." Chandler laughed...

"Mommy – pass me your drink..."

"Here Starr..."

"Ooohhh... it's good..."

"You can't have one..." I laughed...

"I know..."

"Here's to new beginnings..." Chandler said as he raised his glass...

"To knew beginnings..." we all said in unison and then we drank...

"Okay – look at the menu under pasta and pick what you want..." Chandler said... "If you don't want the pasta you can pick chicken, veal, lab, steak, or fish...

"Okay..." Wayne said...

"Here are your appetizers and salads – may I take your dinner order?"

"I'll have the Filetto Di Manzo..." Starr said...

"I'll have the Lombata Di Vitello..." I said...

"Chandler – you wanna help me eat the Bistecca Florentina Per Due?" Wayne asked...

"Porter House? Okay..." Chandler said...

"I'll be back shortly - enjoy your salads and appetizers..." the waiter said as he went to place our order...

"Okay Starr – try the caviar..." Chandler said as he took some, spread it on a cracker, and gave it to her...

"Hmmm... it's not bad..." she said...

"You want some more?" Chandler asked...

"No, no..." Starr laughed. We started eating our appetizers and salads and Chandler spoke...

"So Wayne... you hear anything yet?"

"I did..." Wayne smiled...

"Okay... what's up?"

"I got a job..."

"Already?"

"Yea..."

"Congratulations Dad..."

"Thank you Starr..."

"Where?" Chandler asked...

"UPS..."

"Nice – good pay – good benefits – so you're staying in Canada?"

"We're staying in Canada..." Wayne said as he took my hand, looked at me, and smiled...

"Can I ask you something?"

"Sure..."

"What made you come back?"

"I never stopped loving Mary..." Wayne said as he took my hand and looked at me...

"That's sweet..."

"Thank God Beautiee reached out to me..."

"Beautiee?"

"Yea... she reached out to me in facebook..."

"Dad – you're in facebook?"

"Yes..."

"Oh wow – I'm gonna request you as a friend!" Starr squealed...

"So Beautiee reached out to you? What'd she say?"

"She told me Mary wasn't happy..."

"At first I was mad when Wayne told me..." I said...

"Why Mommy?"

"I thought she was up to something..."

"She was..." Wayne said...

"What do you think she was up to?" Chandler asked...

"You have Starr... she has Bazil... Beautiee just wanted us to have a second chance... and now... we have it..." Wayne said as he looked at me and smiled...

"Yes... we do..." I sighed...

"Aww... Beautiee got y'all back together..." Starr said...

"You hear from the insurance company?" Chandler asked....

"We did..."

"What'd they say?"

"We're getting a check sometime this week..."

"Oh so you gotta leave the hotel?"

"No – we can stay there until we find a place..."

"Okay..."

"I'm happy for you Mommy – now I don't have to worry about you and Dad..."

"No you don't..." Wayne said...

"You hear from Vanessa?"

"We did..."

"You got it?" Starr squealed...

"We don't know yet... but we put in an offer..."

"Hmmm... I'm happy for y'all..." Chandler said...

"We really are celebrating..." Starr said...

"Yes we are..." I said as the waiter came with our plates...

"Oh my God – there's so much food!" I laughed...

"Don't worry – we'll take it back to the room and put it in the fridge..." Wayne said as he looked at me and smiled...

"Aww... you're in love..." Starr said...

"So are you..." I said...

"Yes... we are..." Starr sighed...

"Okay Chandler – ready?"

"Are you ready?" Chandler laughed as he split the porter house between the two of them...

"So Chandler – tell me how you met..." Wayne said as we ate...

"I was sitting in the diner with one of my men having coffee..."

"One of your men?"

"I'm a Sergeant with the Bridgeport Police Department..."

"No shit!"

"No shit!" Chandler laughed... "Anyway...
I'm sitting in the diner having coffee and I saw
Starr at the bus stop..."

"Oh wow..."

"So I got up from the table, I went outside,
I asked her to have coffee with me, and she said
yes..."

"Aww..."

"We would up having dinner, I offered to
take her home, and she said yes..."

"You knew he was the one... didn't you?"
Wayne asked Starr...

"Yes... I knew I wanted to be with him..."
she sighed. Chandler took her hand and kissed
it...

"How'd you propose?"

"I asked her father to come to my house
and told him to wait there while I went to go get
Starr. I told him how much I loved her and I
asked for his blessing – when he gave me his
blessing I proposed right there..."

"Aww man... that's beautiful..."

"It was so romantic..." Starr sighed...

"How old are you Chandler?" Wayne
asked...

"I'm 40..."

"That explains it..."

"Explains what?"

"You're a sergeant – you have to put in
time to become a sergeant..."

"Yes you do..."

"Starr – you did good…"

"Thank you Dad…"

"You ever been married before?" Chandler asked…

"Nope…"

"Why?"

"I met Mary when I was 18… I fell in love with her… I never wanted anyone else…"

"Wayne…" I whispered with tears in my eyes…

"Aww…" Starr said…

"I was tired of going from woman to woman… I asked God to send me a wife… and then I met Starr…" Chandler said…

"Aww… I love you Chandler…" Starr sighed…

"I love you too…"

"So Dad – how'd you propose to Mommy?"

"I didn't do anything fancy… I just took out the ring and asked your mother to marry me…"

"Aww… that's romantic…" Starr said…

"That wasn't romantic…" I said…

"Mommy! Don't say that!"

"After I said yes Wayne told me he had a surprise for me and showed me the tickets to Canada…"

"Ooohhh you bought the tickets before she said yes?" Starr asked…

"Yes…"

"You knew she would say yes?" Chandler asked…

"To be hones... I was scared..." Wayne said...

"Why?"

"I was scared she wouldn't leave..."

"You put your heart out there... and Mary didn't break it..." Chandler said...

"I couldn't let him get away..." I sighed...

"I love you..." Wayne said as he kissed me...

"I love you too..."

"Tell me about your wedding..." Starr said...

"We went to city hall, we got our marriage license, Ms. Woody asked if I had any questions, I asked if we could get married right away, and she married us..." I answered...

"Y'all got married the same day?" Chandler asked...

"Yes..."

"You didn't want a big wedding Mommy?"

"All I wanted was Wayne..." I sighed...

"Ms. Woody kept laughing at us..." Wayne laughed...

"Why?" Starr asked...

"We kept kissing before she could pronounce us husband and wife..."

"I hear that!" Chandler laughed...

"Can I get you anything else?" the waiter asked as he came to the table...

"Oh no – we're good..." Chandler answered...

"How was everything?"

"Everything was delicious..." Chandler answered...

"Glad to hear it – I'll be back with your check..." the waiter said as he walked away...

"So do you have plans for the rest of the week?" Chandler asked...

"Well... I've been looking online and there's a few things I'd like to do..." I answered...

"Like what?" Chandler asked...

"It's a lot..."

"Tell me..."

"Okay – I want to take the ferry to Toronto Island..."

"We can do that – what else?"

"I want to go to the Monkey's Paw – it's a bookstore with items printed from the 20th century and it has a book vending machine..."

"Oh wow – that sounds nice!" Starr said...

"Okay – what else?"

"I want to go to the Thomas Fisher Rare Book Library, the Casa Loma Castle, the Winter Garden Theatre, the Allan Gardens Conservatory, and the Bruce Peninsula Grotto Sea Cave..."

"Umm... Wayne?"

"Yes Chandler?"

"You writing this down?"

"I don't have to – I know my wife – she printed it from the computer..." Wayne laughed...

"Oh – I almost forgot – there's one more thing I wanna do – and I need your help Chandler..."

"Okay – what is it?"

"I'll tell you later..." I answered as the waiter came with the check...

"Aaight – I'ma pay this and we can go..." Chandler said as he got up and went to pay the check...

"I'm so happy..." I sighed as Wayne put his arm around me...

"So am I..." Wayne said. Starr smiled at us as we walked outside.

"Thank you again Chandler – I had a nice time..." Wayne said...

"You're welcome – I had a nice time too..." Chandler said. The uber came, Wayne opened the door for us, we all got in, and went back to the hotel. When we got out the uber, we hugged each other and said good night...

"Chandler?" I called out...

"Yes Mary?"

"I'll talk to you after coffee..."

"Okay Mary – good night..." Chandler said as we all went to the elevator, got on, got off, and went to our rooms...

"I love you Mrs. Robinson..." Wayne said as he kissed me...

"I love you too..." I breathed...

"So..." he said as he kissed my neck... "What's going on between you... and Chandler?"

"I'll tell you tomorrow..."

"Let's go to bed..." Wayne breathed as he kissed me again...

"Mmm.... Okay..."

"I'm so happy..." Starr sighed...

"I'm glad you're happy..." Chandler said as he pulled Starr into a kiss...

"Wayne really love's Mommy..."

"And Mommy really loves Wayne..." Chandler said...

"I wonder what Mommy needs your help with?"

"We'll find out tomorrow..."

"Let's go to bed... I'm tired..." she yawned.

Chapter 5

"Good morning..." Chandler yawned as he answered the phone...

"Good morning Chandler – I know it's early – but can you meet me downstairs in the dining room?"

"Okay – give me a few minutes..."

"Who's that?" Starr yawned...

"Your mother..."

"You're going downstairs already?"

"Yea..."

"I'm coming with you..." Starr said as she got up...

"Starr..." Chandler said as he pulled her into a deep, passionate kiss..."

"Mmmm... you keep kissing me like that I won't let you leave..."

"Let me go downstairs and see what your mother needs help with... give me about 15 minutes... then come down..."

"Okay... but I'm gonna punish you..."

"You promise?" he asked as he pulled her close to him and held her...

"Yes... I promise... now let go before I make you call my mother and tell her you're not coming..." she laughed...

"Who were you talking too?" Wayne asked...

"Chandler..."

"Why so early?"

"I need his help..."

"Come here Mary..." Wayne commanded...

"Yes Daddy?"

"Get back in this bed..."

"I can't..."

"You can... and you will..." Wayne commanded as he sat up and held me close to him...

"Wayne... I need to go..." Wayne stood up, grabbed me by the back of my head and kissed me hard...

"You don't need to go..." he breathed as he reached between my legs... "You need... to stay..."

"Wayne... give me about 15 minutes... then you can come downstairs..."

"Okay... I'll let you go... but I'm going to punish you... for leaving me..." he growled as he kissed me and grabbed my ass...

"I can't wait..." I breathed...

"Good morning Mary – I made you some coffee – what's going on?" Chandler asked as I hurried into the dining room and over to the table...

"Thank you Chandler – I need to make this quick – Wayne doesn't want to let me out of his sight..."

"Your daughter didn't appreciate it either..." Chandler laughed...

"I want to surprise Wayne and buy him this..." I said as I showed him the picture of the Mazda...

"Oh that's nice – you need me to come with you?"

"Yes – and I need you to drive it..."

"You can't drive?"

"It's a manual – I only know how to drive an automatic..."

"Oh... okay – you go on their website and check this out?"

"Yea – it's loaded, no accidents, non-smoker owned – and it's certified..."

"How many miles does it have on it?"

"122,000 km..."

"That's a lot Mary..."

"I know – but it's a 2013 – it's in good condition – and the price includes a 3-year warranty..."

"Okay – that sounds good – how much they askin'?"

"$4,600..."

"You know that doesn't include the license, registration, and taxes right?"

"Yea..."

"How much you got?"

"$5,000..."

"I don't think you have enough – they have any other cars?"

"They have a 2013 Kia Rio LX for $3990 – but it has 175,000 km – and it doesn't come with a warranty..."

"Okay – I'll go over there with you and we'll see what we can do..."

"Thank you Chandler..."

"You're welcome – so you need me to drive it to motor vehicles for you?"

"No – I want you to drive it back here – Wayne can drive us over to the Vehicle License Office..."

"How long does it take to get there from here?"

"It's about 40 minutes if we take the Ontario 401 Express..."

"Okay – I'll go with you – then I'll drive it back here – then we can go with you over there..."

"Thank you Chandler..."

"You're welcome..."

"Good morning Chandler..." Wayne said as he joined us at the table and I put my phone away...

"Good morning Wayne..."

"Good morning Mommy..." Starr said as she came into the dining room and joined us at the table...

"Good morning Starr..."

"You still need Chandler's help? Is there anything I can do?" Wayne asked as he kissed my neck...

"Yes there is..." I laughed... "You can have breakfast with us... and then you can wait here with Starr until we get back..."

"Okay... c'mon Chandler – let's get our wives some breakfast..." Wayne said as he got up, waited for Chandler, and they both went to get us breakfast...

"Why can't we go Mommy?"

"You'll find out when we get back..."

"Oh so you want me to stay here with Dad?"

"Yes..." I answered as they came back to the table...

"I'll be right back – I need coffee..." Wayne said as he got up to go get coffee and Chandler followed. When they came back to the table they set the coffee down and we started eating. Starr looked at Wayne, Wayne looked at me, and they both looked at Chandler. I could tell by the way Wayne was looking at me that he was going to punish me good...

"You ready Mary?" Chandler asked...

"Yes Chandler..." I answered as I got up...

"Okay – we'll be back..." Chandler said as we left them in the dining room...

"Well... looks like it's just you and me kid..." Wayne said as he patted Starr on her head... and she started crying...

"Starr... oh my God... What's wrong... ssshhhh..." Wayne said as he put his arm around her and put her head on his shoulder..."

"You used to call me that all the time..." she sniffed...

"I know..."

"I didn't know what to do when you left..." she cried...

"Starr... I'm sorry..." Wayne whispered as he started crying...

"I thought you hated me..." she cried...

"I could never hate you..."

"Mommy was in jail... I had to go down to the welfare... I lost my job... I needed you..." she cried...

"Starr... I had no idea you were going through that... I'm so sorry..." Wayne cried as they hugged each other...

"If Mommy didn't put me on her Section 8 I don't know what I would've done..." she cried...

"I'm sorry... I didn't mean to hurt you..."

"When you left me you hurt me!" she cried...

"I'm sorry..." Wayne cried... "Please forgive me..."

"I forgive you... I love you..."

"You still love me?"

"Well... I hated you for a long time... but yea... I still love you..."

"You had every right to hate me..."

"Why'd you leave me?"

"I left because... your mother broke my heart..." Wayne whispered as he continued crying...

"Mommy broke your heart?"″

"Yes..."

"She cheated on you?"

"She lied to me..."

"About me?"

"Yes..."

"So... you didn't know Bazil was my father?"

"No..."

"Why did Mommy do that?"

"Your mother didn't mean to hurt me... she knew I wanted children..."

"I'm sorry Dad..."

"You have nothing to be sorry for..."

"You really love Mommy..."

"Yes... I always have..."

"Mommy loves you too..."

"I know..."

"I'm glad you didn't hate me..."

"I could never hate you..." Wayne said as he hugged Starr really tight...

"Dad?"

"Yes?"

"I can't breathe!"

"Oh… sorry…" he said as he let her go…

"Dad?"

"Yes Starr?"

"Are you okay with me having a relationship with my father?"

"Of course…"

"Are you going to talk to my father?"

"Maybe one day…" Wayne sighed…

"I hope you get the house…"

"You do?"

"Yea – then we can come visit…"

"C'mon – let's go out front and find out where your mother is…" Wayne said as he put his arm around her and they walked out to the front of the hotel…

"Hello Starr!" Amy exclaimed… "How are your parents doing?"

"They're fine… and happy…"

"That's good to hear… will you be back at work soon?"

"If things keep going the way they are… I'll be back soon…"

"Okay – I'm glad everything's okay – I'll see you soon…"

"Okay – bye Amy…"

"Who's Amy?"

"My supervisor…"

"Oh…"

"I work at the University of New Haven…"

"Oh wow – how'd you get that job?"

"Chandler got it for me…"

"That's nice!"

"Guess what else?"

"What?"

"Amy's son went to the Police Academy with Chandler – he's a sergeant too…"

"I see…"

"Amy was really worried when I told her about the fire…"

"You told her?"

"Yea… I like talking to Amy – she always makes me feel better…"

"Well that's nice…"

"Good morning – is Angelo here?" I asked…

"Good morning – I'm Angelo – how may I help you?"

"Hi Angelo – I'm here to buy my husband a wedding gift…"

"Congratulations! When did you get married?"

"We were married last week Monday…" I answered as I wrapped my arm around Chandler and pulled him close to me…

"Nine days married and she wants to buy you a car – you're a lucky man…" Angelo said…

"Yes I am…" Chandler said as he hugged me back and played along…

"So… what were you interested in?"

"Im interested in the 2013 Mazda 3 GX..." I answered...

"That's a nice car! I wish my wife would buy me a Mazda! You got any sisters?" he laughed...

"No..." I sighed...

"Damn – that's too bad – c'mon – excuse me – what's your name?"

"Chandler..."

"C'mon Chandler – let me show you your new car..." Angelo said as he walked us over to the car...

"Oh I like this Honey..." Chandler said...

"Here's the keys – take it for a test drive..."

"Okay – c'mon Honey..." Chandler said...

"Coming Dear..." I said...

"I just need one of you to leave your license with me..."

"I'll leave mine since he's driving..." I said as I gave Angelo my license...

"Oh wow – you're a long way from home..."

"We live here now..." I said...

"Oh... okay... I'll talk to you when you get back..." Angelo said as we got in the car and drove off the lot...

"Wayne's gonna like this..." Chandler said as he drove..."

"You think so?"

"Hell yea! I like it!"

"I love him so much..."

"I know... he loves you too..."

"You like him?"

"He's alright... so far..." Chandler said as we drove back into the lot...

"Welcome back!" Angelo said as we got out the car...

"Thank ya..." Chandler said...

"So... you like it?"

"I do..."

"So... you'll take it?"

"I'll take it..." I said...

"Great! Now – I have to let you know – the price doesn't include the taxes, registration, and licensing fees..."

"Angelo – le'me holla at you a sec..." Chandler said as he pulled Angelo over to the side and put his arm around him...

"Chandler – you're a nice guy – but I'm in business to make money..."

"I know... but you don't have to charge the taxes, registration, and licensing fees... if you don't want to..."

"Okay – I'll work wicha – if your wife's paying cash – I'll only charge her for the taxes – she can pay the registration and licensing feels when she goes to the Vehicle License Office..."

"Thank you Angelo – I appreciate that..." Chandler said as he shook his hand and I smiled as they both walked back over to me...

"Mary – I know how much you want to give your husband this car as a wedding gift so I'ma work wicha – if you're paying cash I'll only charge you taxes – you can pay the registration and licensing fees when you go to the Vehicle License Office…"

"Thank you Angelo!" I squealed as I threw my arms around his neck and hugged him…

"Woa! I don't want your husband getting jealous!" Angelo laughed…

"I'm sorry – here's my debit card…" I said as I took out my debit card and handed it to him…

"Okay – that's $4,600 plus the tax – that comes to $$4,968 – okay?"

"Okay!" I squealed…

"Thank you Honey…" Chandler said as he pulled me into a hug and kissed me on the cheek…

"You're welcome Honey…" I blushed…

"Okay – here's your card – I'll process the paperwork – get you the title – and you'll be on your way – you're a lucky man Chandler…" he said as he got up to process the paperwork…

"Thank you Chandler…"

"You're welcome…"

"I can't wait for Wayne to see it…"

"He's gonna really like it…"

"I hope so…"

"Here ya go…" Angelo said as he handed me the paperwork and the keys…

"Here ya go…" I said as I handed the keys to Chandler…

"Thank you Honey..." Chandler said as he opened the door for me and I got in...

"Have a good day Chandler!" Angelo said as Chandler got in, started the car, and drove off...

"Yes Starr?" I laughed as I answered my phone...

"Hi Mommy – where are you?"

"We're on our way back now..." I answered as Chandler laughed...

"Okay... bye Mommy..." Starr said as she hung up...

"You know we in trouble – right?" Chandler laughed...

"I know..." I sighed. When we pulled up in front of the hotel, Starr and Wayne were waiting...

"Oh wow – this is nice!" Starr squealed as we parked and Chandler got out...

"Nice car..." Wayne said as Chandler walked up to him with the keys in his hand...

"Surprise..." I said as Chandler held out the keys...

"Mary... you bought this... for me?"

"Yes..."

"I love you!" Wayne yelled as he picked me up in his arms and spun me around...

"I love you too..."

"So that's why Mommy needed your help..."

"Wayne – take these keys!" Chandler laughed...

"Okay – sorry..." he said as he put me down and took the keys...

"Congratulations Dad..." Starr said...

"Thank you Starr..."

"So... you ready?" Chandler asked...

"Ready for what?"

"Ready to take us out!" Chandler laughed...

"Sure – get in..." Wayne said as Chandler opened the door for Starr, waited for her to get in, and then got in himself...

"C'mere Mary..." Wayne breathed as he pulled me close to him and then he whispered in my ear... "I'm gonna punish the hell outta you..."

"We leavin'?" Chandler laughed...

"Yea... we're leavin'" Wayne said as he opened the door for me, waited for me to get in, and then got in himself... "Where to?" Wayne asked...

"Let's go to the Monkey's Paw Bookstore downtown..." I said...

"Okay... Wayne said as we headed downtown to the bookstore. We spent a good part of the day in the bookstore and then we went to the Gabardine for lunch... "Oh this is a nice lil' spot..."

"I like it..." Starr said... "I see what I want right here – mac' n' cheese, herbed breadcrumb toast – with smoked ham..."

"I'ma go with the buttermilk battered fried chicken thigh, with graham's red hot sauce..." Chandler said...

"I'ma go with the bacon cheeseburger, thousand island, tomatoes, lettuce, & fries..." Wayne said...

"You getting' a cheeseburger?" Chandler asked...

"You can tell a lot about a place by their cheeseburgers..." Wayne said...

"I'll get the bacon cheeseburger too..." I said...

"We stayin' here or goin' back to the hotel?" Chandler asked...

"We can stay here..." Wayne answered...

"Welcome to the Gabardine – have a seat anywhere you like – I'll bring you your menus..." the waiter said as we sat down and he went to get menus...

"Here ya go..." the waiter said as he put the menus on the table...

"We already know what we want..." Wayne said...

"Okay – what'll you have?" the waiter asked...

"Two bacon cheeseburgers, a buttermilk battered fried chicken thigh, and mac' n' cheese – with ham..." Wayne answered...

"Okay! What can I get ya ta drink?"

"Alcohol!" Wayne laughed...

"Sir – we don't serve alcohol until after 3 p.m...."

"Really? Okay – how about ice tea?"

"Sweetened or unsweetened?

"Sweetened..."

"Okay – four sweetened ice teas coming up..." the waiter said as he went to get our drinks...

"Starr was telling me you got her the job at the University..." Wayne said...

"I did..."

"She also told me you went to the police academy with her supervisor's son..."

"Yea... Jeremy..."

"Starr say's Amy's really nice..."

"She is Dad..."

"Yea – Jeremy's mother is really sweet..." Chandler said...

"Here's your lunch..." the waiter said as he brought our foot to the table...

"Ooohhh... this looks good..." Starr said...

"It does – can I taste your mac' n' cheese?" I asked...

"Sure Mommy..."

"How's your chicken Chandler?" Wayne asked...

"He's not talking – that means it's good!" Starr laughed....

"Right..." Chandler laughed...

"This burger is delicious!" I exclaimed...

"We might be back here..." Wayne said as we finished eating. "I'll get this one Chandler..." Wayne said as he got up to pay the check...

"Thank ya..." Chandler said.

"Where to now?" Wayne asked...

"Let's walk to the Thomas Fisher Rare Book Library since its close by..." I said...

"Okay..." Wayne said as he took my hand and we all walked to the library. We spent the next hour looking at all the rare collections of books and then we walked outside and walked around the university...

"I'm ready for a nap..." Starr yawned...

"We can go back to the hotel now if you want..." Wayne said. We walked back to the car, got in, went back to the hotel, and got in the elevator...

"Maybe we'll see you later tonight?" Chandler asked...

"Maybe..." Wayne answered...

"We'll call you..." Chandler said...

"Okay... talk to you later..." Wayne said as we got off the elevator and went to our rooms.

Chapter 6

As soon as Wayne closed the door I knew I was in for it... "Come here..."

"Yes Daddy..." I breathed as I walked over to him. Wayne took his time undressing me and then he stood back to look at me...

"Turn around..." he commanded. I turned around and he came up behind me, pulled me close to him, and smacked my ass...

"Ooohhh..." I moaned...

"Sit down..." Wayne commanded as he led me over to the bed...

"Yes Daddy..." I breathed. I watched Wayne get undressed and he stood in front of me, fully erect... "Open your mouth..." he commanded as he put his hand on the back of my neck and pushed me towards his dick... "Show me your tongue..." Wayne commanded. I stuck my tongue out and Wayne put the tip of his dick on it... "Lick it..." he commanded. I licked the head of his dick, swirling my tongue from top to bottom, tasting his pre-come...

"Like that Daddy?"

"Yes Mommy.... Just like that..." Wayne breathed...

"May I?" I asked as I took his dick in my hand and started stroking it...

"Yes Mommy... yes you may..." he breathed as I took his dick in my mouth and sucked it while continuing to stroke it... "Yes Mommy... suck it..." Wayne moaned. I took his dick deeper into my mouth and Wayne stopped me... "Mommy... stop..."

"Yes Daddy?" I asked as I looked up at him...

"Get on your back..."

"Yes Daddy..." I breathed as I got on my back. Wayne spread my legs, bent them at the knees, and held them in place as he looked down at me...

"Mommy... your pussy is so pretty..."

"Thank you Daddy..." I breathed...

"You ready for Daddy?"

"Yes Daddy... yes..." I moaned. Wayne held my legs open, tilted me up, and eased himself in my ass... "Oh God..." I moaned...

"You okay Mommy?" Wayne asked as he pushed his dick in further...

"Yes Daddy..." I moaned...

"You want Daddy to fuck you?"

"Yes Daddy... yes..." I moaned. Wayne started fucking me slowly as he held my legs in place... "Ooohh... Ooohhh... Ooohhh..."

"You like my dick Mommy?"

"Oh yess…" I moaned…

"Mommy… you feel so good… ughh…" Wayne moaned as he started fucking me faster…

"Oohhh… yes Daddy…. fuck my ass…"

"Play with your pussy Mommy…"

"Oh yes… you gon' make me come Daddy…" I moaned as he fucked my ass and I played with my pussy….

"Yes Mommy… I love watching you play with your pussy while I'm fucking you…" he growled as he grabbed my legs and pulled me all the way down on his dick…

"Huh… huh… huh…"

"Yes Mommy… Ugghhh…"

"Daddy… Fuck… I'm about to come…" I moaned as I swirled my fingers around my clit faster…

"Yes Mommy… cum for me…"

"Aaagh… Aaagh… Aaagh… Aaagh…"

"Uugh! Uugh! Uugh! Uugh!"

"Aaaahhhhh!" I screamed as my body jerked and I rubbed my clit harder…

"Yes Mommy… was it good?"

"Yes Daddy… yes…" I breathed as I continued playing with my pussy…

"Mommy… Fuck… I'm cumming… Uuuggghhhh!" Wayne growled as he thrust his dick in my ass…

"You like that Daddy?" I breathed…

"Mmmmm…. Yes Mommy…" he breathed as he spread my legs, laid down on me, put his tongue in my mouth, and tongued me down as he fucked my ass some more...

"Hmmmph... you givin' it to me good Daddy..." I moaned...

"Oh yea? You like how Daddy fucks your ass?"

"Yes Daddy..." I moaned...

"Mmmm..." Wayne moaned as he kissed me again..." I love it when you're naughty..." he breathed...

"So do I..." I breathed... "I wanna watch you..."

"You wanna watch me?"

"Yes Daddy..."

"Okay Mommy..." he breathed as he got up off me and went into the bathroom. When he came back, he wiped his dick off with a wash cloth and then he started stroking himself... "Like this Mommy?"

"Yes Daddy..." I moaned as I started playing with my pussy again...

"Spread your legs Mommy... I wanna see your pussy..." Wayne growled as he stroked himself...

"Yes Daddy..." I moaned as I spread my legs and continued playing with my pussy...

"Yes Mommy... le'me see... Uuggh!"

"Yes Daddy... Like that..."

"You like this Mommy?" Wayne breathed as he stroked himself faster...

"Yes Daddy... ooohhh..."

"Mommy... I'm cumming..."

"I'm cumming with you Daddy... Aaagh... Aaagh..."

"Uugh! Uugh! Uugh! Uugh!"

"Aaagh... Aaagh..."

"Uuuugh!"

"Yes Daddy... cum in my mouth..." I moaned as I arched my back, opened my mouth, and came all over my hand as Wayne shot in my mouth. Wayne lifted my head, put his dick in my mouth, and watched me suck his dick as he moved my hand and started playing with my pussy with his hand... "Mmmph... Mmmph... Mmmph..." I moaned on his dick. Wayne pushed his dick in my mouth and swirled his fingers around my clit faster... "Mmmph! Mmmph! Mmmph! Mmmph!" Wayne was getting hard in my mouth and I sucked him harder as he played with my clit harder... "Mmmph! Mmmph! Mmmph! Mmmph!" I grabbed Wayne's dick with my hand and jerked him off in my mouth as I came again... "Mmmph! Mmmph! Mmmph! Mmmph!"

"Uuugh! Uuugh! Uuugh! Uuugggghhhh!" I swallowed every drop and then I took his dick out my mouth...

"Like that Daddy?"

"Yes Mommy... just like that..." Wayne said as he sat up on the bed, pulled me up, and kissed me...

"Now…" Chandler said as he closed the door, locked it, and pushed Starr up against it… "You said something earlier… about punishing me?"

"Yea…" she sighed…

"Uh uh…" Chandler said as he pulled her into a hug… "What's wrong?"

"This morning… after you left… Dad called me kid…"

"Aww…"

"Chandler… it made me cry…"

"Starr… come sit with me…" Chandler said as he took her over to the bed and they sat down… "Why were you crying?"

"Dad used to always say looks like it's just you and me kid…"

"Oh…"

"I told him I thought he left 'cause he hated me…"

"Starr…" Chandler whispered as he held her… "That's not why he left…"

"I know…"

"You do?"

"He told me he could never hate me because he loves me…"

"Aww…"

"I told him everything I went through and he cried…"

"Oh wow…"

"I told him when he left, he hurt me…"

"I know he hurt you Starr… I'm sorry…"

"He told me he's sorry and he asked me to forgive him…"

"Do you?"

"Yea…"

"Good…"

"I asked him why he left me and he said Mommy broke his heart…"

"She cheated on him?"

"No – she never told him about my father…"

"Oh so he always thought you were his daughter?"

"Yea… he said Mommy didn't mean to break his heart – she didn't tell him because she knew he wanted children…"

"How do you feel about that?"

"I understand…"

"You do?"

"Yea…"

"You needed to have that talk…"

"Yes we did…"

"And he needed you to forgive him…"

"I know…"

"I'm starting to like Wayne…"

"You didn't like him?"

"I didn't trust him…"

"Oohhh. So you trust him now?"

"He's alright…"

"So… about your punishment…" Starr said as she stood up… "Since you helped my mother and made her so happy…" she said as she took off all her clothes and got in the bed... "I'm not going to punish you... I'm going to reward you..."

"Oh... okay..." Chandler said as he stood up, took off all his clothes, and climbed in bed with her... "What's my reward?"

"Anything you want..." she breathed...

"Anything?" Chandler asked...

"Anything..." Starr whispered.

"Well..." Chandler said as he pulled her into a kiss... "I already have everything I want..."

"Oh Chandler..." Starr whispered as she kissed him...

"Do you remember the first time you saw me in my uniform?" he asked as he kissed her...

"Yes..." she said as she kissed him...

"You said I was looking good..." he said as he kissed her...

"You were..." she said as she kissed him...

"I said maybe I should'a wore it the first night you met me..." he said as he kissed her... "and you said you were glad I didn't..."

"Because..." she said as she kissed him... "I got to fall for the man behind the uniform..." she said as she climbed up on top of Chandler and kissed him again...

"And now..." Chandler said as he kissed her... "We're having a baby..." Chandler said as he moved his hands down her back to her ass and pushed her down on his dick. Starr put her tongue in Chandler's mouth and they tongued each other down as Chandler held her ass and pushed his dick up inside her...

"Hmmph...   Hmmph...   Hmmph... Hmmph..."

"Mmmph...   Mmmph...   Mmmph... Mmmph..." Chandler flipped Starr over on her back, spread her legs, put his tongue in her mouth, and fucked her deeper...

"Hmmph...   Hmmph...   Hmmph... Hmmph..."

"Mmmph...   Mmmph...   Mmmph.... Mmmph..." Starr lifted her legs up and dug her nails into Chandler's ass as she pushed him in deeper and Chandler knew she was close to cumming...

"Hmmph...   Hmmph...   Hmmph... Hmmph..."

"Mmmph...   Mmmph...   Mmmph... Mmmph..." Starr's moaning intensified as her legs shook and Chandler didn't let up...

"HMMPH!   HMMPH!   HMMPH! HMMPH!" Chandler lifted Starr's legs and fucked her harder as he came inside her...

"MMMPH!   MMMPH!   MMMPH! MMMPH!" Starr locked her ankles around Chandler's back and held him as their orgasm's subsided and they continued kissing...

"Hmmph...   Hmmph...   Hmmph... Hmmph..."

"Mmmph...   Mmmph...   Mmmph... Mmmph..."

"Hmmph...   Hmmph...   Hmmph... Hmmph..."

"I'ma have to keep you pregnant..." Chandler breathed...

"Why?" Starr breathed...

"Because..." Chandler breathed as he kissed her... "Your pussy..." he said as he started thrusting again... "is so fuckin' good..." and then he put his tongue in her mouth and tongued her down as they went for round 2...

"Hmmph...   Hmmph...   Hmmph... Hmmph..."

"Mmmph...   Mmmph...   Mmmph... Mmmph..."

"Hmmph...   Hmmph...   Hmmph... Hmmph..."

"Mmmph...   Mmmph...   Mmmph... Mmmph..."

Chapter 7

"Mommy..." Wayne whispered as he kissed me awake...

"Yes Daddy?" I yawned...

"Here... take a look at this..." Wayne said as I sat up and looked at his laptop...

"Ooohhh... this is beautiful..." I said as I looked at photos of the CN tower...

"We can sit at The 360 Restaurant and enjoy panoramic views of Toronto – as long as we get a seat by the window..."

"I wanna go..."

"Okay – I'll make reservations..." Wayne said as he took the laptop and made reservations for us...

"I'll call Starr..."

"Hi Mommy..."

"How'd you know it was me?" I laughed...

"I didn't..." she laughed...

"Listen – Wayne's making reservations for us at The 360 Restaurant..."

"Where's that?"

"It's in the CN tower..."

"Ohhh... we can take pictures..."

"Yes we can..."

"What time?"

"Hang on – Wayne – what time?"

"7 o'clock..."

'Wayne says 7 o'clock..."

"Okay – I'll tell Chandler..."

"Be downstairs at 6:30..."

"Okay Mommy – see you later..."

"Hi Dad..."

"Hey Starr – Le'me speak to Chandler..."

"Dad wants to talk to you..." Starr said as she handed Chandler the phone...

"Hey Wayne..."

"Hey – listen – can you meet me downstairs at the bar for a drink?"

"Sure... I'll be right down..."

"Where are you going?"

"I'm going to meet your Dad downstairs..." Chandler said as he kissed Starr and then headed downstairs to the bar...

'Drinks with Chandler?" I asked...

"Yea..."

"Oh boy..."

"I'll be back soon..." Wayne said as he kissed Mary and then headed downstairs to the bar...

"You're here..." Wayne said when he saw Chandler...

"I'm here..." Chandler said...

"What'll it be?" the bartender asked...

"Two Henneys – on the rocks..." Wayne answered...

"Okay Wayne – what's this about?" Chandler asked as the bartender put the drinks on the table...

"Why'd you come up here?"

"Why do you think I came up here?"

"I have an idea – but I want you to tell me..."

"I came up here for Starr..."

"I know that's one reason... but that's not the only reason..."

"Her mother is very important to her – which makes her important to me..."

"I like that..." Wayne said...

"I don't really know you... but Starr does..."

"I know..."

"She loves you – and you hurt her... I didn't like that..."

"Understood..."

"I'm glad you and Mary are happy and I'm glad you and Starr had that talk..."

"Oh so she told you?"

"Yea – she told me – you gon' have to earn my trust..."

"I know..."

"It's gonna be a minute..."

"That's okay..."

"You ready for another?" the bartender asked...

"Yes sir..." Wayne answered...

"Two Henneys – coming up..." the bartender said...

"Starr asked me if I was ever going to talk to her father..."

"Le'me stop you right there – that's between you and him..."

"I know he's your father-in-law..."

"Like I said – whatever happens between you and him is between you and him..."

"Understood..."

"When we first started dating I didn't know she was Bazil's daughter..."

"You didn't?"

"Nope..."

"Oh wow – I bet that was an awkward conversation..."

"It was – but we got past it..."

"That's good..."

"It's only been a few days – and now that you're staying in Canada – it's gonna be a few more before we can get past this..."

"Understood..."

"So far, I know you love Mary, I know you love Starr, and I know Starr doesn't have to worry about her mother..."

"Thank you Chandler..."

"Thanks for the drinks – I need to put in some quality time with my wife before we go out to dinner – I'll see you later..." Chandler said as he got up...

"Okay Chandler – I'll see you in a bit..." Wayne said as he got up and they both left the bar...

"Everything okay?" Starr asked...

"Everything's okay..." Chandler answered...

"What'd he want?"

"Nothing serious..." Chandler answered as he got undressed, got back in bed, and snuggled up under Starr...

"You're back..." I said...

"I'm back..." Wayne sighed...

"That was quick..."

"It was..."

"You okay?"

"Yes Mary..."

"No you're not... what happened?"

"Chandler wasn't really interested in talking..."

"Aww... don't take that personal..."

"I have no choice but to take it personal..." he sighed...

"Wayne... come here..." I said as I held my arms out. Wayne got undressed, got in bed, and let me hold him... "You don't need to try so hard..."

"Yes I do – I..." I interrupted Wayne with a kiss... "I love you Mary..."

"I love you too..."

"Starr told Chandler about our talk..."

"Your talk?"

"This morning – after you left – we talked... we cried... and I asked her to forgive me..."

"Did she?"

"Yes..."

"Aww... that makes me happy..."

"It makes me happy too..."

"Chandler will come around... but you need to give him time..."

"That's basically what he said...

"So..." I said as I pulled him down on top of me... "How much time do we have before dinner?"

"We have a little over an hour..." Wayne answered as he started massaging my breasts...

"Ohhh... that's plenty of time..." I breathed...

"Plenty of time..." he breathed and then he started licking my nipples... "For what?"

"For whatever... you want..." I breathed...

"Mmmmm...." Wayne moaned as he kissed his way down my stomach... "I like the sound of that..." he said as he put his hand between my legs and pushed his fingers inside me... "and..." he said as he moved down between my legs and spread my lips... "From what I can tell..." he said as he flicked his tongue on my clit... "You like the feel of it…" he said and then he began sucking my clit while finger-fucking me…

"Haaa…. Haaa…. Haaa…. Haaa…."

"Ready for dinner?" Wayne asked as Starr and Chandler came downstairs…

"Yea – we ready…" Chandler answered…

"Okay – I'll be right back…" Wayne said as he went to go get the car…

"How you feelin'?" I asked as I pulled Starr into a hug…

"I'm okay Mommy – I'm just tired…"

"That's to be expected…"

"Oh because I'm pregnant?"

"Yes…"

"Okay – car's outside…" Wayne said as he motioned for us to come outside. We all got in the car and Wayne drove off. The sun had started to go down and it was really pretty. When we got to the CN Tower, Starr was excited…

"Oh look – it's so nice!"

"It does look nice…" Wayne said as he parked the car. Wayne and Chandler got out, opened the door for us, and we stood there for a moment admiring the sunset… "Let's take a selfie in front of the tower…" Wayne said as he took out his phone and we all got together for the selfie. We went inside and thank God we had a reservation because the line was long…

"Do you have a reservation?"

"Yes – Robinson – party of four…" Wayne answered…

"Okay – come with me…" the host said as we followed him to the upper level and he walked us over to a table by the window…

"This is nice – thank you Wayne…" Chandler said…

"You're welcome…" Wayne said as he smiled…

"Chandler – I wanna get a picture by the window…" Starr said as she got up…

"Okay…" Chandler said as he followed her. I watched as chandler put his arms around Starr and hold her and it made me smile…

"Mrs. Robinson?"

"Yes Mr. Robinson?"

"Will you take a picture with me?" he asked as he stood up and extended his hand…

"Yes…" I answered as I got up. Wayne took my hand and led me over to where he wanted to take our picture. Wayne held me and prepared to take a selfie and I could see Starr taking a photo of us at the same time. When we were done, we went back to the table and the waiter was there to take our orders…

"Welcome to 360 – may I start you off with something to drink?"

"I'd like a bottle of the 2017 Chardonnay Blend aka Follow The White Rabbit…" Wayne said…

"Ooohhh.... I love Chardonnay..." Starr said...

"Very well – I'll be back..." the waiter said. When he came back to the table, he opened the bottle and poured each of us a glass...

"Here's to us..." Wayne said as he raised his glass...

"To us..." we all said and then we took a sip...

"May I have your order for appetizers?' the waiter asked...

"I'll have the Ocean Wise Champion Seafood Chowder..." I said...

"I'll have the 360 Charcuterie..." Starr said...

I'll have a Caesar Salad..." Chandler said...

"I'll have the wild BC Sockeye Salmon Tartare..." Wayne said...

"Okay – I'll be back in a few..." the waiter said...

"This Chardonnay is really good..." Starr said...

"It is good..." I agreed. The waiter came back to the table with our appetizers and Chandler's salad and was ready to take our orders...

"That was fast..." Chandler said...

"Thank you sir..." the waiter said... "Are you ready or do you need a few more minutes?"

"I'll have the Ballotine of Ontario Chicken Caprese..." Starr said...

"I'll have the Coast To Coast Shrimp Cavatelli..." I said...

"We'll have the 10 oz AAA Roast Beef Prime Rib – right Chandler?" Wayne asked...

"Right..." Chandler answered...

"I'll be back shortly..." the waiter said as he went to place our orders...

"This is so good!" Starr exclaimed...

"Everything tastes good to you lately..." Chandler laughed...

"That caviar didn't taste good!" Starr laughed...

"This is good..." Wayne agreed...

"You can't really mess up a Caesar Salad..." Chandler said...

"I'm enjoying mine..." I said...

"I notice your appetite for seafood has picked up..." Wayne said...

"My appetite for good seafood never went away..." I laughed. The waiter brought our dinner to the table just as we finished our appetizers and Chandler finished his salad...

"Ooohhh! I don't know if I can eat all this!" Starr laughed...

"If it's as good as your appetizer was... our child will help you finish it..." Chandler said as he took her hand and kissed it..."

"Aww... look at them..." Wayne said...

"I bet you acted like this with Mommy..." Starr said as we started eating...

"He did..."

"Yea... I did..." Wayne laughed...

"We all did when we were younger..." Chandler said. We spent the rest of the evening eating and taking pictures until the restaurant was about to close, and then we got up to leave. When we got downstairs and went outside the sky was beautiful...

"I'm so sleepy..." Starr yawned...

"We gonna get you back to the room so you can go to bed..." Chandler said as he wrapped his arm around her...

"C'mon – let's get back so we can all go to bed..." Wayne said as we went to the car, got in, and Wayne drove off. When we got back to the hotel, Starr was asleep in the back seat...

"Starr..." Chandler whispered as he kissed her awake...

"Yes Chandler?" she yawned...

"We're here..."

"Oohhh... okay..." she yawned. Chandler got out the car, opened the door for her, and helped her out the car...

"C'mon Mary..." Wayne said as he opened the door and extended his hand for me to take so he could help me out the car. We all went inside the hotel and got in the elevator...

"Good night y'all..." I yawned before we got off..."

"Good night..." they said in unison...

"Good night Starr... good night Chandler..." Wayne said...

"Good night..." they said in unison again as we went to our room...

"Thank God..." I said as Wayne put the do-not-disturb sign out and closed the door...

"You okay?"

"Yes Wayne – I'm okay – I just wanna get comfortable..." I said as I took off my clothes and got in the bed...

"I'd like to get comfortable too..." Wayne said as he took off his clothes and got in bed beside me...

"Tomorrow's Thursday..." I sighed...

"Yes it is..." Wayne said as he pulled me under his arm and I laid on his chest...

"I wanna go home..." I sighed...

"I wanna go home too..."

"You do?"

"Yea..."

"I'm glad it's not just me..."

"It's not..."

"I just wanna wake up, go in my kitchen, and make you coffee..."

"Or vice versa..."

"I want a bed like this..."

"We can get one..."

"I can't wait to decorate..."

"Me too..."

"Really?"

"Yes – starting with that ugly carpet..." Wayne laughed...

"What – you don't like dirty carpet?" I laughed...

"I hope we hear from Allstate tomorrow so I can call Vanessa..."

"I hope so too..."

"Thank God they have HSBC Banks here..."

"They do?"

"Yea – so I won't have to close my account..."

"That's good..."

"Once I start working, my payroll is direct deposit so it'll be a smooth transition..."

"I can't wait..."

"Neither can I..."

"I wonder if they have Lazy Boy here in Canada?"

"They have lazy Boy... and Ethan Allan..."

"Oh good – I'll be able to get top-of-the-line..."

"Mary?"

"Yes Wayne?"

"We gotta be easy..."

"Wayne?"

"Yes Mary?"

"We need a bed that won't collapse when we're fucking..." I laughed...

"True..." Wayne laughed...

"As for the rest of the furniture – we need stain-resistant..."

"Why? We don't spill food and drinks..." Wayne laughed...

"Remember when I got drunk and threw up all over the couch?"

"Oh yea... I forgot about that..."

"Plus – the baby will spit up, spill juice..."

"The baby?"

"Our grandchild..."

"Wow..." Wayne whispered...

"You okay?"

"You said our grandchild..."

"Yea... I did..."

"I love you..." Wayne breathed as he kissed me...

"I love you too..." I yawned as we fell asleep.

Chapter 8

"I can't wait to get the island..." I said...

"Me either..." Wayne said as he kissed me. When we got to the island, the first thing I wanted to do was walk around but Starr had another idea...

"Let's go to the Girbraltar Point Lighthouse!" she said excitedly...

"Okay..." Chandler said...

"No the hell you will not!" I laughed...

"Excuse me?" Chandler asked...

"The Gibraltar Point Lighthouse was built in 1808..." I said...

"So what?" Chandler asked...

"It's haunted!" I snapped...

"Le'me find out you're afraid of ghosts..." Chandler laughed...

"I'm sorry Chandler – as long as Starr is carrying my grandchild she's not going anywhere that's haunted..."

"Mary..." Wayne said as he touched my shoulder...

"I said no!"

"Okay Mommy – I won't go in there..."

"Come here..." Wayne laughed as he pulled me into a hug...

"No..." I said as I struggled to get out of his arms to no avail...

"If it upsets you this much, we won't go..." he said as he kissed me...

"Can we walk past it?" Chandler asked...

"Yea – but I'm not stopping in front of it..." I said. When we got to the Great Lakes I could see the lighthouse in the distance. Starr stopped to take pictures...

"It sure is pretty..." she said...

'It's pretty – as long as we stay over here and the lighthouse stays over there..." I laughed. We continued walking until we got to the Labyrinth of Evergreens William Meeny Maze...

"How 'bout this Mommy?" Chandler mocked... "Is this okay?"

"Actually – it may make us sick..." I answered...

"How Mary?" Wayne asked...

"It's a maze so we're going to get dizzy – Starr might throw up..."

"So we can't go in there either?" Starr asked...

"We can go – but if you start to feel nauseous just come outside..." I said as we all went into the maze...

"Ohhh... it's beautiful..." Starr said as we walked around...

"You alright Mary?" Wayne asked...

"I feel like I'm drunk!" I laughed as I fell into Wayne...

"Ooops... I gotcha..." Wayne laughed...

"Uh oh... I'm gonna be sick..." Starr said...

"Hang On Starr... we're almost done..." Chandler said as he started rubbing Starr's back...

"Don't look up Starr... just look straight ahead..." I said and as soon as we got out the maze, Starr threw up... "Welcome to motherhood..." I laughed...

"Is this what morning sickness is?" Starr asked...

"Yea..."

"How long does it last?"

"Sometimes it can last the whole pregnancy..." I answered as we continued walking...

"Did you have a lot of morning sickness?"

"Naa... you just had me eating all the time..." I laughed...

"Speaking of eating – who's eating with me?" Wayne asked as we walked over to the Toronto Island BBQ & Beer Co. "Oh me – I want a mac n' cheese burger!" Starr exclaimed...

"I'ma have some smoked beef back ribs..." Wayne said...

"Me too..." Chandler said...

"I'll have a mac n' cheese burger..." I said as we went inside...

"I know we can get a few beers here..." Wayne said as we sat down...

"I want a beer..." Starr sighed...

"You can have a beer Starr..." I said...

"Uh uh!" Chandler snapped...

"Relax Chandler..." I laughed... "Starr can have an Oduls – its non-alcohol..."

"Okay – she can have one of those..." Chandler laughed. After about an hour or so we left the restaurant and went to the Far Enough Farm on Centre Island.

"Oh Look – they're so cute!" Starr said as we went over to the mini pot belly pigs...

"Some people keep them as pets... "Wayne said..."

"No thank you..." Chandler laughed. After we walked through the farm and saw all the other animals I saw something I wanted to try and I got really excited...

"Oh – I wanna get naked at Hanlan's Point!"

"What?" they all asked in unison...

"I wanna go to Hanlan's Point Beach, I wanna go where the clothing is optional, I wanna take off my clothes, and I wanna go swimming... with you..." I said as I put my arm around Wayne...

"Okay..." Wayne said as he smiled...

"I'on wanna see that!" Chandler laughed...

"Me either!" Starr laughed...

"You don't have to..." I laughed... "You can stay on the other end of the beach where clothing is mandatory..." I said as I took Wayne's hand and we walked to the beach. "Okay – we'll be back in a bit – bye!" I said as I pulled Wayne towards the clothing optional beach... "I can't wait to get outta these clothes..." I breathed as I undressed...

"I can't believe we're doing this..." Wayne breathed as he took off his clothes...

"I'm so excited – when we get in the water I wanna go deep – and I want you to fuck me in the water..." I breathed...

"Okay..." Wayne breathed as he took my hand and we ran into the water...

"Oh yes... this feels so good..."

"It does feel good..."

"Finally – a moment away from the kids..." I laughed...

"You're right..." Wayne said as he grabbed me around my waist and I wrapped my legs around him... "I can't believe I'm fucking you in public..." Wayne growled as he thrust himself up inside me...

"Yes Wayne... Fuck me..." I moaned as I wrapped my arms around his neck and fucked him back...

"You're so turned on... and so am I..." Wayne breathed as he fucked me under the water...

"I'm cumming..." I moaned...

"I'm cumming with you…"

"Fuck me Wayne…"

"Ugh! Ugh! Ugh!"

"Hah… Hah… Hah…"

"Uuuugh!"

"Aaaagh!"

"Oh shit… Fuck…" Wayne breathed…

"I wanna do this again…"

"So do I…" Wayne breathed as he pulled me to him and kissed me hard…

"I hope they had fun…" I laughed…

"I don't give a fuck if they had fun or not…" Wayne breathed…

"Let's take a nude selfie on the beach before we get dressed…" I said as I picked up the phone, tried to take a selfie, and dropped it…

"Hi there – need some help?" the man asked…

"Sure – thanks…" Wayne laughed…

"Okay – stand over here…" the man said as we posed and he took the picture of us…

"Aww… look Wayne…" I said as I showed him the picture…"

"Thanks man…" Wayne said…

"You're welcome…" the man said as he walked off…

"Let's get dressed and go find Chandler and Starr…" Wayne said…

"Okay…" I said as we got dressed and went to the other side of the beach… "Hey!" I said as we walked up to them…

"Did you have fun?" Chandler laughed...

"We sure did!" Wayne answered as he pulled me into a kiss...

"Did you really get naked and go swimming Mommy?"

"Mmmm Hmmm..." I moaned as Wayne held me and we continued kissing...

"Let's go to Electric Island – the next show starts at 2 o'clock..." Chandler said...

"You wanna go Mary?" Wayne asked...

"Yesss..." I breathed... "I wanna go..."

"Okay... let's go then..." Chandler said as he took Starr's hand, Wayne took my hand, and we spent the afternoon dancing to a variety of music. When the show was over I wasn't ready to leave so I suggested another activity...

"Let's take a swan ride..."

"A swan ride?" Starr asked...

"Yea – it's right outside Centerville's theme park – we get in a boat and the guys pedal the boat around the pond..." I said...

"Sound's good..." Wayne said...

"Sounds romantic..." Starr said. Wayne got a boat for us, Chandler got a boat for them, and we rode around the pond. When we were done with that Starr suggested another activity...

"Let's play Frisbee golf!"

"That sounds like fun..." I laughed as we walked over to Wards, got a couple of Frisbees, and spent the next hour playing Frisbee golf on the 18-hole course...

"Whew... I'm tired!" Starr breathed...

"Me too..." I laughed...

"Too tired to eat?" Wayne asked...

"I ain't that tired..." I said as they all laughed...

"Whathca have in mind?" Chandler asked...

"I was thinking about the New Orleans Seafood & Steakhouse..." Wayne answered...

"That sounds good..." Chandler said...

"Alright – let's go..." Wayne said as we followed him to the car and we got in..."

"I hope I'm not sore tomorrow..." Starr said...

"You're the one that wanted to play Frisbee..." I laughed...

"At least it was fun..." Starr said...

"It was..." Wayne agreed. We all looked out the window and admired the sunset as Wayne drove to the New Orleans Seafood & Steakhouse...

"This is cozy..." I said as we went inside and sat down...

"They even have oil paintings and instruments on the wall to make it authentic..." Chandler said...

"I hope the food's not too spicy..." Starr said...

"If you don't want anything spicy, go with the coconut beer shrimp..." I said...

"Okay Mommy..."

"Welcome to New Orleans Seafood & Steak – what can I get for you?" the waiter asked...

"Two orders coconut beer shrimp..." I said...

"Caesar salad..." Chandler said...

"I'll take a spinach salad..." Wayne said...

"And what would you like to drink?"

"I'd like a ginger ale..." Starr said...

"I'll have that too..." I said...

"I'll have Guinness..." Chandler said...

"Make that two..." Wayne said...

"Okay – I'll be back shortly..." the waiter said as he left to place our orders. When he came back to the table with our drinks, their salads, and our shrimp, Starr's eyes got wide...

"Oh my God – they're so big!"

"Go ahead honey – try one..." I said as we started eating...

"Oh my God Mommy – they're so good!"

"Told ya!" I laughed as we finished eating and the waiter came back to the table...

"Are you ready to order dinner?"

"Yes – I'll have the chicken creole pasta..." I answered...

"What? You don't want the seafood creole pasta?" Wayne asked as he felt my head... "Where's my wife?" he laughed...

"Mommy – what's in the chicken creole pasta?"

"That's smoked chicken, mushrooms, and spinach in a creamy creole sauce Maam..." the waiter answered...

"Okay – I'll have that too..." Starr said...

"We gon' have the Black Angus steak..." Chandler said...

"Both of you?" the waiter asked...

"Yes sir!" Wayne answered...

"May I refill your drinks?" the waiter asked...

"Yes please..." I answered...

"Very well... - I'll be back..."

"Coconut shrimp is good..." Starr said...

"It's one of my favorites..." I said...

"I wonder how you make it?"

"Same way you make fried shrimp – just have a cup of coconut so you can dip them in the coconut after you dip them in the flour..."

"Ohhh... that's easy – I'ma make these at home – and invite Theresa over..."

"Who's Theresa?" Wayne asked...

"Our neighbors – Theresa and Charles..." Chandler answered...

"Here's your drinks – I'll be right back with your dinner..." the waiter said as he placed the drinks on the table...

"I'd like to meet them..." I said...

"You will – after the baby's born – I'm sure they'll be right up under us!" Starr laughed...

"Here's your dinner – if you need anything else – just ask..." the waiter said as he placed our food on the table...

"Starr – when are you due?" Wayne asked...

"Probably February..."

"Probably?"

"Yea – I haven't been to the doctor yet..."

"Why?" I asked...

"We just found out Mommy..." Starr laughed...

"True – but don't wait – go as soon as you get home..."

"Beautiee says I should go to Dr. Julianne..."

"I agree – but Dr. Julianne doesn't deliver babies..."

"That's what Beautiee said..."

"You and Beautiee are pretty close – huh Starr?" Wayne asked...

"Yea..." Starr sighed...

"I'm glad you have a good relationship with her – especially since she's responsible for getting us back together..."

"So how's Jay?" I asked, even though I could honestly care less...

"He's fine – he's getting big..." Starr answered...

"You have any pictures of your lil' brother Starr?" Wayne asked...

"Yup – le'me pull one up for you…" she answered excitedly…

"How's your steak Wayne?" Chandler asked…

"This is actually the best steak I've had since we've been here…" Wayne answered…

"Here Dad – here's a good one…" Starr said as she handed her phone to Wayne…

"Oh my God – he looks just like Bazil!"

"Yes he does…" I agreed…

"My son is going to look just like Chandler…" Starr sighed…

"My son will be beautiful no matter who he looks like…" Chandler said as he pulled Starr into a kiss…

"Aww…" Wayne said…

"Beautiee says I'm eating for two – or three…"

"How does she know? Is she a doctor?" I snapped…

"I'm sure she didn't mean anything by it…" Wayne said as he kissed me…

"You're right – Beautiee might be a sensitive like you Starr…" I said…

"She is Mommy…"

"Shit – if you're having twins, it's a good thing we have a guest room – I'ma need your Momma to move in for a couple a weeks…" Chandler said…

"Aww… thank you Chandler…" Starr sighed…

"Thank your Momma!" Chandler laughed...

"Can I come?" Wayne laughed...

"Hell yea – one baby for each of you – Starr's gonna need her rest!" Chandler laughed...

"I'm coming to stay even if you only have one child..." I said...

"My children are lucky..." Starr said...

"Yes they are!" Chandler laughed...

"My babies will have two grandmas... and two grandpas...

"Yes they will..." Wayne said as he put his arm around me...

"Starr – how's your food?" I asked, trying to change the subject...

"It's good Mommy..."

"Not too spicy?"

"Nope..."

"That's good – between spicy food and heartburn I had to keep crackers in the house..."

"Was it bad Mommy?"

"Yes chile – and you were born with a head full of hair..."

"Oh so my babies are gonna be born with hair like mine..."

"Or mine!" Chandler said as he rubbed his bald head and we all laughed...

"Anybody have room for dessert?" Wayne asked...

"Naa..." Chandler answered...

"I don't..." Starr answered...

"Me either..." I answered...

"Okay then – let's go..." Wayne said as he got up...

"They didn't bring the check yet..." Starr said...

"Don't worry – they'll have it up-front..." Wayne said as we got up from the table and he went to pay the check. Chandler, Starr, and I followed behind and after he paid the check, we went outside, got in the car, and Wayne drove us back to the hotel. As soon as we got in the lobby Starr couldn't wait... "Good night Mommy – good night Dad – I'm tired..." she yawned as she hugged us both...

"Good night kid..." Wayne said as he kissed her on her forehead...

"Good night Starr..." I said...

"Good night Mommy – good night Dad..." Chandler said as he gave us a bear hug...

"Good night Chandler..." I got out as best I could...

"Good night Chandler..." Wayne said...

"Excuse me – Mr. Robinson?" the lady behind the front desk called out...

"Yes Maam?" Wayne answered...

"This was delivered for you while you were out..." she said as she handed Wayne an envelope from Allstate...

"Thanks..." Wayne said as he took the envelope, put it in his pocket, we all went to the elevator, and got it...

"Good night guys..." I said as we got off the elevator...

"Good night..." they said in unison as we went to our room. As soon as Wayne closed the door he opened the envelope and smiled...

"You got the check..." I sighed as I smiled...

"We got the check..." Wayne said as he pulled me into a kiss...

"We're going home..."

"Yes Mommy.... We're going home..."

"I can't wait for you to call Vanessa!" I said excitedly...

"You won't have to..." Wayne said as he picked up his phone and dialed her number...

"Vanessa Garcia speaking..."

"Hello Vanessa – it's Wayne – I'm sorry to be calling so late..."

"Real Estate doesn't stop of 5 o'clock – I was up anyway – what can I do for you?"

"We got the check..."

"That's great!"

"I would have called you earlier but we've been out all day..."

"That's fine – I'll come get the check in the morning..."

"You don't need me to deposit the check?"

"Nope – all you need to do is sign it – I'll deposit it – and it'll be in escrow until we close – which will be in a couple of days – you're not getting kicked out of the hotel are you?"

"No – we can stay here up to 30 days…"

"You won't need to – I'll see you late tomorrow morning or early afternoon…"

"Thank you Vanessa…" Wayne said as he hung up…

"What'd she say?" I asked excitedly as I took my clothes off…

"She's coming to pick up the check tomorrow – I sign it – she deposits it – it stays in escrow until we close…" Wayne answered as he took his clothes off. Wayne walked over to me, put the check on the table, pulled me close to him, and started kissing me on my neck…

"Oh Daddy…" I moaned…

"Yes Mommy…" he breathed in my ear as he nibbled on my ear lobe…

"We're going home…" I breathed as I wrapped my arms around his neck…

"We're going home…" he said as he picked me up and I wrapped my legs around him…

"We're going home…" I said as he carried me over to the bed, fell down on top of me, and we both fell asleep.

Chapter 9

"Wayne..." I whispered as I shook him awake...

"What's wrong?" he asked as he jumped up...

"There's somebody at the door..." I whispered...

"Oh shit!" Wayne said as he jumped up, threw on his robe, and went to look out the peep hole...

"It's Vanessa – Hold on Vanessa..." Wayne said as I jumped up, threw on my robe, and Wayne opened the door... "Come on in..."

"I'm sorry – I tried to call – you didn't answer – the clerk at the front desk tried to call – she said the line was busy..."

"No need to apologize – I'm sorry we didn't hear the phone..." Wayne said...

"Oh my God – the phone's off the hook..." I said as I put the phone back on the receiver...

"I know how anxious you are to get this place – otherwise I would've just left a message..."

"Vanessa – please... sit down..." Wayne said as he pulled out a chair for her to sit...

"Thank you for understanding..."

"Here – le'me sign this and give it to you right now..." Wayne laughed as he took the check out the envelope, signed it, and gave it to Vanessa..."

"Thank you – now we can get things moving along – I'm going to get this to the bank right now – I'll call you later today..." she said as she put the envelope in her purse and got up to leave...

"Thank you again Vanessa..."

"You're welcome – and again – I'm sorry..."

"Stop apologizing!" Wayne laughed as he opened the door before Chandler and Starr could knock on it...

"Well good morning!" Chandler beamed...

"Good morning – nice to see you – I need to get going – Wayne – I'll call you later..." Vanessa said as she hurried to the elevator...

"Can we come in?" Starr asked as she walked in and Chandler followed...

"You're already in here..." I laughed as they both sat down in the chairs and we sat on the bed...

"We just woke up..." Starr laughed...

"So did we..." Wayne laughed...

"We tried to call you..." Chandler said...

"Yea – the phone was off the receiver..." I said...

"We tried to call your cell too..." Starr said...

"I gotta check my phone – I didn't even hear it ring..." Wayne said as he picked up his phone to look at it...   "It's not charged – no wonder it didn't ring..." he laughed...

"Wow – you must've been really tired..." Starr laughed...

"We still are..." I yawned...

"We're hungry..." Chandler laughed...

"Well... we missed breakfast..." I sighed...

"I guess we could get dressed and then we can all go to the Mystic Muffin..." Wayne said...

"Okay – we'll go back to our room – call us when you're ready..." Chandler said as he got up... "C'mon Starr..."

"Okay..." Starr said as she got up and followed Chandler out the room... and Wayne bust out laughing...

"What's so funny?" I asked...

"They probably think we were in here fucking!" he laughed...

"We could be..." I said as I walked over to him, took his dick in my hand, and started stroking it...

"Mary... the kids... are... hungry..." he breathed...

"So am I..." I said as I laid back on the bed and spread my legs...

"Oh... you're gonna get it..." Wayne said as he got on top of me, put my arms above my head, eased himself inside me, and started fucking me hard...

"Yes Daddy... Fuck me..."

"Is this what you want?" he growled...

"Yes! Fuck me!"

"Uggh! Uggh! Uggh! Uggh!"

"Aagh! Aaah! Aaagh! Aaaaaggghhh!"

"Uggh... Fuck... I'm cumming... Uuuugggghhh!"

"Shit..." I breathed...

"I love it when you wanna fuck..." Wayne breathed as he kissed me...

"And I love it when you fuck me like that..." I breathed as I kissed him back... and then the phone rang...

"Hi Starr..." Wayne answered...

"Hi Dad – are you coming?"

"Yes Starr – your Mom just got out the shower – give us a few more minutes..."

"Okay..."

"I guess I better get in the shower..." I laughed as I got up out the bed and went towards the bathroom and Wayne followed...

"Wayne..."

"I know, I know – it'll be faster if be both get in at the same time..." he said as he turned on the shower and we both got it...

"Hello Conrad..."

"Hello Bazil..."

"How's everything?"

"Everything seems to be okay…"

How's my son-in-law enjoying his second honeymoon?"

"I haven't heard anything…"

"Hmmm… he must be enjoying himself…"

"I have something for you…"

"What's that?"

"She bought a car…"

"Did she?"

"Yes…"

"Was it expensive?"

"No…"

"Does she have any money left?"

"No…"

"Does he?"

"He has a couple a thousand – that's about it…"

"Any unusual activity?"

"Nothing outta the ordinary – just a few debits for restaurants…"

"No other activity?"

"Not yet – I'll probably see something by the end of the week…"

"Keep me posted…"

"I will…"

When we got downstairs Starr had her arms crossed and she was pouting…

"We're here…" I said…

"I'm mad at you!" She snapped…

"Aww... don't be mad Starr..." Wayne said...

"Oh please – you'll get over it..." I laughed...

"You think this is funny?" Chandler asked...

"You'll get used to her tantrums – trust me..."

"I'm not having a tantrum – I'm mad!" she snapped...

"C'mon Starr – let's go eat – you'll feel better..." Chandler said as he put his arm around her and we went out to the car and got it. Chandler held Starr's hand as she continued to pout until we got to the restaurant and got out...

'I can't wait to get some coffee..." I said as we went inside... "Oh look – they were voted Best Breakfast..."

"Sit anywhere you like..." the owner said... "I'll be right with you..." We sat down and looked around at how busy they were and started looking at the chalk boards...

"Good morning – can I start you off with some coffee?"

"Oh God – yes!" Starr exclaimed...

"Yes Maam..." he laughed as he poured us all coffee...

"Sugar, creamer, milk, etc. – right in the corner – now – what can I get you to eat?"

"I'll have the down east breakfast sausage, mushroom, spinach, & onion quiche..." I said...

"I'll have the buck's bacon and farm egg, English muffin with white cheddar..." Chandler said...

"Make that two..." Wayne said...

"Okay – I'll be right back..." the owner said as he left a pot of coffee in the middle of the table and went to place our orders...

"So Vanessa came to see you earlier..." Chandler said as we all started drinking our coffee...

"Yes..." Wayne said...

"Any news?" Chandler asked...

"We got the check..." Wayne answered as he took my hand and kissed it...

"Congratulations..."

"Thank you Chandler..."

"Congratulations..." Starr mumbled...

"Thanks kid..." Wayne said as he patted her head and pulled her into a hug. Starr tried not to smile but she couldn't help it...

"When y'all closing?"

"Sometime next week..." Wayne answered...

"Oh so you'll still be in the hotel when we leave?" Starr asked...

"Yes Starr..." I answered...

"I wish we could be there when you get the keys..."

"That would be nice... but I know you have to get back to work..."

"Daddy was at the closing with me when I got my keys…"

"He was?"

"Yea – we both had to sign a lot of papers…"

"Both of you had to sign?"

"Yea – the co-op is in both our names…"

"Oh that's nice – maybe your father will turn it over to you later on…" Wayne said…

"Here's your breakfast – if you need anything else…"

"Actually – there is something else…" Wayne interrupted…

"Okay – what'll it be?"

"Bring us some of that apple cake everyone raves about…" Wayne said…

"Okay – I'll bring that over in a few…" the owner said…

"This is really good – a man's sandwich…" Chandler said…

"Yes – a man's sandwich…" Wayne agreed…

"How's your quiche Mommy?"

"Delicious…"

"You feel better now?" Chandler asked…

"Yea… I was hungry… and cranky…" Starr answered…

"That's okay – I still love you…" Chandler said and then he kissed her…

"I love you too Chandler…"

"Here's your apple cake…" the owner said as he put our plates on the table…

"Ooohhh… this looks good!" Starr said as she took a piece with her fork and tasted it…

"Well? How is it?" Chandler asked…

"Mmmmm…." Starr moaned as she slid down in her chair while rubbing her stomach…

"That good huh?" Wayne laughed….

"It's good!" Chandler said as he tasted his…

"I see why it gets rave reviews…" Wayne said as he ate his…

"Oh my God – it's delicious!" I said as I ate mine…

"I see you're enjoying the cake…" the owner laughed…

"Mmmmm Hmmmmm!"

"Uh huh…"

"Oh yea…"

"Yeesss…."

"Glad to hear it – I'll be back with your check…" the owner said as he went to get our check…

"The food here is really good – we gotta come back…" Starr said…

"Yes we do – and we'll have lunch instead of breakfast…" Wayne said…

"What're we doing today?" Chandler asked…

"I wanted us to go to the Casa Loma – it's a castle with 98 rooms…" I answered…

"Oh Wow – I don't know if I can walk that much..." Starr said...

"We'll see when we get there..." I said...

"Don't worry Starr – we can take a break whenever you want..." Wayne said...

"Okay... I'll go..." she said as she stood up...

"Good..." Wayne said as he put his arm around her waist and pulled her close to him... "Because every castle needs a princess..." he said as he kissed her on the cheek...

"Aww... thank you Dad..."

"You're welcome – let's go..." Wayne said as we got up and walked over to the register...

"Leaving so soon? I hope it wasn't anything I said..." the managed laughed as he handed Wayne the check...

"Oh that's funny!" Wayne laughed as he handed the manger his debit card....

"Thanks for coming in – come back soon..."

"We will..." Wayne said as we went out to the car and got it...

"It sure is beautiful here..." Starr said...

"It is... in the summer..." Chandler said...

"I'm glad we didn't wait to come here..." I said as I took Wayne's hand...

"So am I..." Wayne said. When we got closer to the castle you could really see how big it was...

"I hope they have an elevator..." Starr said...

"I don't think so – but it's only three floors…" I said…

"Let's take some pictures outside…" Wayne said as he parked the car and we got out. When we got to the front of the castle there were lots of people taking pictures so I volunteered myself…

"Hi – listen – we'd like to take a few pictures - how 'bout I take some pictures of you with your phone and you take some pictures of us with our phone – okay?"

"Sure miss – we can do that…" the lady said…

"Honey – she's gonna take some pictures of us and we're gonna take some pictures of them…" she told her husband…

"Okay Dear…" he said as he handed me their phone and I took some pictures of them… "Thank you Maam – now I'll get some pictures of you with your family…"

"Thank you sir…" Wayne said as he handed the man his phone…

"Is this your wife?" the man asked as he started taking pictures…

"Yes – this is my wife, this is our daughter, and this is her husband…" Wayne answered as he introduced us…

"Well you have a lovely family – get in here so I can get some pictures of you together…" he said. We all stood together and had a picture taken… "Okay Lil' Lady – you come over here with your husband so I can get a picture of you by yourselves..."

"Okay..." Starr smiled as she went in front and Chandler pulled her into a kiss...

"Got it!" the man said as he handed the phone back to Wayne...

"Thank you..." Wayne said...

"You're welcome..." the man said... "Yall have a nice day..." he said as he put his arm around his wife and they went inside the castle...

"They were really nice..." Starr said...

"They were nice..." Chandler agreed...

"Let's go to the third floor – then we can work our way down..." Wayne said...

"Good idea..." I said as we went inside and followed everyone upstairs...

"You okay Starr?" I asked...

"I'm okay Mommy..." she said...

"I got her..." chandler laughed as we continued up the stairs to the third floor...

"Whew!" I said when we got to the top of the stairs...

"Tired huh?" Wayne laughed...

"My legs are tired... but I' fine..."

"I'm gonna start taking pictures..." Starr said as she took out her phone. We spent the next 30 minutes taking pictures and selfies in the Group of Seven Room, the Pellatt Board Room, and the Austin Room. When we were done taking pictures we followed everyone down to the second floor... "Oh wow – look!" Starr said as she plopped down on the bed in Lady Pellatt's Suite...

"Starr – get up..." I whispered...

"Chandler – come take a picture with me..."

"Chandler – don't encourage her!" I whispered as he ignored me and got in the bed with her so she could take the picture. Wayne just shook his head and laughed as I threw up my hands...

"C'mon – let's see the rest of the suite..." Wayne said as he took my hand. When we got to Sir Pellatt's Suite Wayne pulled me over to the bed and pulled me down on top of him...

"Wayne! Stop it!" I laughed...

"Got it!" Starr said as she took the picture along with about a dozen other people...

"Oh great – now we'll be all over social media and we won't be allowed back in the castle..." I laughed as I got up...

"You mad at me?" Wayne asked as he came up behind me and kissed me on my neck...

"Naa... but I want that bed..."

"You got it..." he said as we went to the Guest Room, the Rand Room, and then the Windsor Room... "Time to go downstairs..." Wayne said as we finished taking pictures and then we followed everyone downstairs to the first floor. We started in The Great Hall, took some pictures, and then we went into the Library...

"How do they maintain all these books?" Chandler asked...

"Lot of librarians..." Wayne answered...

"And lots of ladders – look how high the shelves go up!" Starr exclaimed. We went to the Conservatory and took some pictures, and when we went to the Terrace and Gardens, Wayne's phone rang...

"Yes Vanessa..." Wane answered...

"I have good news..."

"Okay..."

"Your money's in escrow..."

"Okay..."

"So... the seller doesn't want to wait..."

"Okay..."

"He wants to close right away..."

"Okay..."

"We can close on Monday..."

"Okay..."

"Are you okay?"

"Yes Vanessa..."

"Okay – I'll see you Monday morning – and Wayne?"

"Yes Vanessa?"

"Make sure your phone is on the hook!" she laughed...

'Okay..." Wayne laughed as he hung up...

"Everything okay?" I asked. Wayne didn't answer me – he pulled me into a kiss and held me... "You should get calls like that more often..." I breathed...

"We close on Monday..." Wayne said and then he kissed me again...

"You close on Monday?" Starr asked...

"We close on Monday...' Wayne and I answered in unison and then we kissed again...

"C'mon – we need to get going..." Wayne said as he took my hand and pulled me towards the main entrance...

"Where are we going?" I laughed as Starr and Chandler hurried behind us...

"The Elgin and Winter Garden Theatre..." Wayne answered as he unlocked the door and we got in the car...

"What's at the theatre?" Chandler asked...

"It's actually a pair of stacked theatres – the Winter Garden Theatre is seven stories above the Elgin Theatre – according to Wikipedia, they're the last surviving Edwardian stacked theatres in the world..."

"Sounds nice..." Starr said...

"We're going to see a performance of Come From Away – they'll use visual aids to help us follow along so we know what they're saying... and what they're singing..."

"Sing? You?" I laughed...

"Yes Mary – me..." Wayne answered...

"Why you laughing Starr?" Chandler asked...

"You haven't heard Dad sing!" she laughed...

"Oh this is gonna be fun!" Chandler laughed...

"Can you sing Chandler?" Wayne asked...

"Yeesss...." Starr sighed...

"Oh well – so singing isn't my thing – so what..." Wayne said...

"What's it about Dad?"

"All I know is everyone loves it... and they're all proud to be Canadian..." Wayne answered as we pulled up in front of the theatres...

"Oh I can't wait to take pictures!" Starr exclaimed...

"You'll get some nice ones – wait until we get inside..." Wayne said as we got out the car and went inside...

"Oh wow..." Chandler said...

"I had no idea it was so beautiful..." I said as we all took pictures before the show started...

"Hello Conrad..."

"Hello Bazil..."

"How's everything?"

"He just got his refund deposited into his account..."

"Oh... that's right... he worked last year..."

"The insurance company came through..."

"Good..."

"Yes it is... especially for them..."

"Chandler will be home soon then..."

"Yes..."

"Thank you Conrad..."

"You're welcome Bazil..."

"Oh my God – that was fun!" Starr laughed as we went to the car...

"It sure was!" Chandler laughed...

"Your singing is better than it used to be..." I said...

"Thank you Mary..." Wayne said as he kissed me...

"Why didn't you sing Mommy?"

"I was too busy laughing..." I laughed...

"Did you have a nice time?" Wayne asked...

"I sure did..." I answered as I kissed him...

"It was nice – I'm glad we came – thanks Wayne..." Chandler said...

"You're welcome..."

"Where are we going now?" Starr asked...

"Richmond Station..." Wayne answered as he started the car and we drove off. When we got to the restaurant Chandler and Starr looked around....

"Hmmm – this is a busy spot..." Chandler said as we went to an available booth and sat down...

"Hi guys – I'll be right with ya..." the waiter said as he went to get menus and came back... "Can I start you off with something to drink?" the waiter asked...

"Two Richmond Brown Ale, one Oaxaca Margarita, and Spiced Lemonade..." Wayne answered...

"Okay – are you ready to order?"

"Yes – Four Station Burgers..." Wayne answered...

"Burgers?" Chandler asked...

"Trust me..." Wayne answered...

"Okay..." Chandler said...

"Very well – I'll be back with your drinks..." the waiter said as he went to get our drinks...

"You and your burgers..." Chandler laughed...

"I haven't been wrong yet..." Wayne said...

"True dat..." Chandler agreed...

"Here's your drinks – ales for the guys – a margarita for the lady – and a spiced lemonade for you..." he said as he gave the spiced lemonade to Starr...

"Oooohhh... this is good!" Starr exclaimed...

"This margarita is delicious..." I said as I sipped...

"How's the ale Chandler?" Wayne asked...

"I'm ready for another..." Chandler answered...

"Okay!" Wayne said...

"Here's your burgers..." the waiter said as he placed the burgers on the table... "Can I get you anything else?"

"Two more ales…" Wayne answered…

"Okay – I'll be back…" the waiter said as he went to get the ales…

"This burger is sooo good!" Starr exclaimed…

"It is good…" Chandler agreed…

"I love these fries…" I said…

"I think this is the best burger we've had…" Chandler said…

"Mmmm Hmmmm…" Wayne agreed as he finished his burger and fries…

"I guess you were hungry…" I laughed…

"I was…" Wayne said as he finished his beer…"

What's for dessert?" Starr asked…

"I'll let you know in a sec…" Wayne answered…

"You can tell us now…" Chandler laughed…

"You're not finished…"

"My bad – le'me eat this last bite…" Chandler said as he finished his food…

"How's everything?" the waiter asked…

"Delicious…" Wayne answered…

"Can I get you any dessert?"

"Smores…" Wayne answered…

"Smores? Like when we were kids?" Starr asked…

"Smores…" Wayne answered…

"Okay!" I'll be back…" the waiter said as he went to get our dessert…

"I can't believe they have Smores!" Starr exclaimed...

"Neither can I..." Chandler said...

"I can't wait to taste it..." I said...

"Here ya go..." the waiter said as he put our Smores on the table...

"Oh Damn!" Chandler said as he took a bite...

"Le'me try it..." Starr said as she took a bite... "Ooohhh... this is good!" Starr exclaimed...

"Mmmm Mmmm Mmmm!" I said as I ate mine...

"Mmmm...." Wayne moaned as he ate his. I watched him meticulously as he ran his tongue up and down the ice cream and he smiled at me mischievously...

"Uggh... I'm full..." Starr said...

"I'm good..." Chandler said...

"I could eat another one..." Wayne said as he smiled at me mischievously...

"Can I get you anything else?" the waiter asked...

"Naa... we're good..." Wayne said...

"Okay – here's your check..." the waiter said as he put the check on the table...

"C'mon guys – let's get back to the hotel..." Wayne said as we got up from the table...

"Okay..." Starr yawned. Wayne stopped to pay the check and then we went out to the car and got it...

"You sure you're okay to drive?" Chandler asked...

"I'm okay to drive..." Wayne answered as he started the car and drove off. We all looked out the window as Wayne drove. I smiled to myself as I thought about the closing. Wayne looked over at me and took my hand as he continued driving. When we got to the hotel Wayne parked the car and we took turns groaning as we all got out...

"I can't wait to go lay down..." Starr said...

"You alright?" I asked...

"I'm just tired Mommy..."

"So am I..." I said...

"We had a long day..." Chandler said...

"We had a great day..." Wayne said...

"Yes... we did..." I agreed. We walked into the lobby and went straight to the elevator, and got in...

"Night Mommy, night Dad..." Starr yawned when we got to their floor..."

"Night..." Chandler yawned...

"Night guys..." Wayne yawned...

"Good night..." I said as they got off the elevator and we went to our floor, got off the elevator, and went to our room... "Oh thank God..." I breathed as I got undressed and got in the bed. Wayne got undressed, got in bed beside me, pulled me to him, and began kissing me... "Mmmm..." I moaned...

"Tomorrow's Saturday..." he breathed as he kissed me...

"I know..."

"They leave on Sunday..." he breathed as he kissed me again...

"I know..."

"We close on Monday..." he breathed as he kissed me again...

"I know..."

"We can go back to the beach..." he breathed as he kissed my neck...

"I'd like that..."

"We can come back to the hotel..." he breathed in my ear...

"Yesss...."

"And I can fuck you all day..."

"Oh yes..." I breathed...

"Or all night..."

"Yeess..." I breathed...

"But tonight..." he breathed as he got on top of me... "As I said earlier..." he breathed as he kissed his way down my stomach...

"Yes Daddy..." I moaned as I arched my back and he slid his hands up under my ass and held me up off the bed...

"I could eat another Smores..." he said and then he dove in...

"Huh.... Huh... Huh... Huh... Huh..."

Chapter 10

"Good morning..." Chandler whispered as he kissed Starr awake...

"Good morning..." she yawned...

"Good morning..." he said as he kissed her stomach...

"Ohhh!" Starr exclaimed...

"What's wrong?"

"The baby's moving..." she said as she put his head on her stomach...

"Hey Baby..." Chandler said as he felt the baby moving...

"I'm tired..." Starr yawned...

"You wanna stay in bed?"

"Yea..."

"Okay..." Chandler said as he got up and started getting dressed...

"Where are you going?"

"I'm going to get you some breakfast – I'll be right back..." Chandler said as he hurried out the door and down to the lobby...

"Hey Chandler..." Wayne said...

"Good morning..." Chandler said...

"Where's Starr?" I asked…

"She's staying in bed…" Chandler said as he started making plates…

"Is she okay?" Wayne asked…

"She's okay – she's just tired…" Chandler answered…

"I'm gonna check on her…" I said…

"She's okay…" Chandler said…

"I heard you – but I'm still going to check on her…"

"Okay…" Chandler laughed….

"You want us to take our food and go now?" Wayne asked…

"No – we'll finish breakfast, we'll let them have breakfast, and then we'll check on her…" I answered…

"Okay – I'll let Starr know…" Chandler said as he left with the food…

"Mary?"

"Yes Wayne?"

"She's okay…"

"No she's not…"

"You were tired when you carried her…"

"She's not as far along as I was…"

"Mary…" Wayne said as he took my hand…

"Yes Wayne?"

"She's fine… okay?"

"Okay – she's fine…" I relented as I started eating…

"We'll go check on her okay?"

"Okay..." I sighed as I smiled...

"Starr – come open the door..."

"Okay Chandler..." she said as she got up out the bed and opened the door with nothing on...

"Starr! What if someone was in the hallway?"

"Oh... Sorry..." she yawned. Chandler put the plates on the table and pulled Starr into a hug...

"You sure you're okay?"

"Yes Chandler... I'm just tired..."

"Your mother's coming to check on you..."

"Oh boy – I better put something on..." she said and then she went to put on her pajamas...

"C'mon – let's eat while it's hot..." Chandler said...

"Okay..." Starr said as she ran to the bathroom and Chandler heard her heaving. Chandler got up, went into the bathroom, and held her hair as she vomited. Chandler took a washcloth, wet it with warm water, and began wiping her face with it... "I'm sorry..." she whispered...

"Stop apologizing..." he said as he wet the wash cloth again and wiped her neck...

"That feels nice..."

"Good..." he said and then he picked her face up by her chin and kissed her...

"I love you Chandler..."

"I love you too..."he said as he pulled her up off the toilet and held her...

"Let's go try to eat..." she said...

"Okay – c'mon..." he said as he wrapped his arm around her and led her out the bathroom to the table and sat her down... "You sure you wanna eat?"

"Yea... let me try..."

"Okay..." Chandler said as he sat down and they started eating... and then they heard knocking... "There's your parents..."

"I know..." Starr sighed as Chandler got up to open the door...

"Hi Starr..." I said as I went over to her..."

"Hi Mommy..."

"You okay?"

"I'm really tired..."

"Le'me see..." I said as I felt her head... "Hmmm... you're a little warm..."

"Is that a bad thing?" Wayne asked...

"No – she's not burning up..." I answered...

"Where we goin' today?" Chandler asked...

"Well – I wanted us to take the subway and street car to the Allan Gardens Conservatory..." Wayne answered...

"The Conservatory?" Starr asked...

"Yea – it's a greenhouse that's over 100 years old..." Wayne answered...

"Oh wow..." Chandler said...

"It's over 16,000 square feet..." Wayne said...

"That's a big garden..." I said...

"I'm tired... I wanna stay here..." Starr said...

"Okay..." I said as I hugged her...

"Get some rest..." Wayne said as he hugged her...

"We'll see you later..."

"Okay... bye Mommy... bye Dad..." Starr yawned...

"See y'all later..." Chandler said as he closed the door...

"Chandler... I need to lie down..." she said as she stood up... and fainted...

"Starr!" Chandler exclaimed as he ran over to her, picked her up off the floor, and cradled her in his arms...

"Chandler – open the door!" Wayne yelled...

"I can't!"

"Hey you – get this door open – now!" Wayne snapped at the housekeeper...

"I don't know who the fuck you think you're talkin' to..." she started to say before I interrupted...

"Lady – we need you to open the door..."

"Housekeeping!" She yelled as she banged on the door...

"Come in!" Chandler yelled...

"Okay – I'll open the door..."

"Thank you…" I said as Wayne went in first and I followed…

"C'mon Starr…" Wayne said as he went over to Chandler, picked Starr up, and laid her on the bed…

"What happened?" she asked…

"You fainted…" Chandler answered…

"I'm scared…"

"Don't be scared baby…" I said as I sat down on the bed, took her hand, and rubbed it…

"Why did I faint?"

"Hormones…"

"Hormones?"

"Yea – they make blood vessels relax and widen to increase the blood flow to the baby – but if it doesn't get back to your veins quick enough, you get dizzy, you get lightheaded, or you faint…"

"You sure Mommy?"

"Yes baby – I'm sure…"

"So I don't need to go to the hospital?"

"Are you in any pain?"

"No…"

"Are you bleeding?"

"No…"

"Then you don't need to go to the hospital – but you need to get to a doctor as soon as you get back…"

"I will Mommy…"

"In the meantime – get in bed – and stay in bed – understand?"

"Yes Mommy…"

"Okay – we're gonna go – Chandler – call us if you need us…"

"Okay Mary…" Chandler said as we left…

"That was scary…" Wayne said…

"Once I saw she was okay I wasn't worried…"

"I saw that…"

"I didn't get tired that early – but every pregnancy's different…"

"Okay…"

"Let's go to the Conservatory – Chandler will call us if he needs us – she's in good hands…"

"Yes she is…" Wayne agreed as we got on the subway…

"I'm sorry you didn't get to finish your breakfast…" Starr said…

"Didn't I tell you to stop apologizing?" Chandler said…

"I'm sorry – I mean – I don't know what to say!" she laughed…

"It's okay – I love you…" Chandler laughed as he kissed her…

"I didn't brush my teeth…"

"So what…" Chandler said as he kissed her again…

"Can you get me some coffee?"

"Sure – I'll make us some…" Chandler said as he got up and went to make coffee…

"I really wanted to go to the Conservatory…"

"I know you did…"

"You're not disappointed?"

"Yes – I get to spend the whole day catering to my wife in a nice hotel – just the two of us – and I get to lie on my wife's stomach and talk to our child – oh man – I wish I could've gone with your parents instead…"

"Okay, okay…" she laughed…

"Here…" Chandler said as he handed her a cup of coffee…

"Thank you Chandler…"

"You're welcome – how you feelin'?"

"Well… I'm actually feelin' a little better…" she answered as she finished her coffee…

"Is that right?" he asked as he finished his coffee…

"Mmmm Hmmm…" she nodded as she smiled at him mischievously…

"Hmmm… let me make sure…" Chandler said as he got undressed and got in bed beside her…

"Chandler… that tickles…" she laughed as Chandler nibbled on her neck…

"So…" he asked as he kissed her neck… "Does this hurt?"

"Mmmm… no…"

"Does it feel good?" he breathed….

"Yeessss…."

"Okay…" he breathed as he opened her pajama top and began massaging her breasts… "Does this hurt?"

"Mmmm…. no…"

"Okay… be breathed as he took her right breast in his mouth… "How 'bout this?" he asked before he started sucking…

"Oh… that feels… good…"

"Okay…" he breathed as he got up, got on top of her, and pulled her pajama pants off… "I need to check everything…" he said as he started kissing her down her stomach…

"That feels good too…"

"Okay…" he said before he spread her legs and started licking her clit…

"Huh… Chandler…"

"Does it hurt?"

"No… Huh… Huh…" Chandler started sucking her clit and her moaning intensified… "Huh… Huh… Huh…"

"Mmmm…." Chandler moaned as he licked and sucked…

"Chandler… I'm cumming… I'm cumming… Huh… Huh… Huh… Huh… Huuuuuuuh!" Chandler looked up at Starr, came up from in between her legs, layed down on top of her, and kissed her…

"There it is…" he whispered…

"There what is?"

"Your orgasmic glow…" he answered as he eased himself inside her…

"Oh... Chandler..."

"Yes Starr..." he breathed as he started thrusting...

"This subway sure isn't like New York Subways..." I laughed...

"Amazing – isn't it?" Wayne asked...

"I just can't believe how clean it is..." When we got off at College Station it looked more like New York Subways but it was much cleaner... "No graffiti! No garbage!" I exclaimed...

"Let's go outside..." Wayne laughed as we went out the exit...

"Now this reminds me of New York City..." I said...

"There's the Carlton Street Car..." Wayne said as we crossed the street, waited, and got on. We looked out the window and enjoyed the sights as we rode to the Conservatory. "Oh wow – I don't think we'll be to see it all!" I exclaimed...

"We'll see as much as we can..." Wayne said as we walked around. After about an hour or so I started getting tired... "You ready to go?"

"Yea... I'm ready..."

"C'mon – let's take the Carlton Street Car back to Carlton Street and get something to eat..."

"Okay..." I said as we waited for the street car and got on. When we got off on Carlton

Street I was amazed by all the hotels and restaurants...

"Where would you like to go?" Wayne asked as he pulled me close to him...

"Let's go to Union Jack Fish & Chips..."

"I don't think they have burgers..."

"Please?" I asked as I ran my hand over his crotch and up his chest...

"Okay..." Wayne answered as he smiled at me mischievously. I knew I was in for it and I couldn't wait...

"Welcome to Union Jack – is this your first time here?" the manager asked...

"Yes it is..." Wayne answered...

"We have a special for new customers – sign up for our rewards and get a free appetizer..."

"Okay – we'll sign up..." Wayne said as he filled out the form and I looked at the menu...

"Ooohhh – I see everything I want..."

"Umm... Mary?"

"Yes Wayne?"

"There's only two of us..."

"Starr didn't eat – I wanted to bring extra food in case she's hungry..."

"Oh yea – I remember when you were pregnant – your appetite was bottomless..."

"Which one?" I asked as I threw my arms around his neck and kissed him...

"All of them..." he answered as he kissed me back...

"Aww... I like that..." the manager said as he came over to us...

"Thanks..." Wayne said...

"See anything you like?"

"Yes – I'd like just about everything on your menu..." I answered...

"You sure?" the manager asked...

"Yes..." I answered...

"Okay! What can I get ya?"

"I'll have four seafood platters with chips – no lemon..."

"Okay – what else?"

"I'll have two orders of mac & cheese bites, and two orders of cream cheese poppers..."

"Okay – what else?"

"I'll have two orders of chicken fingers..."

"Okay!" the manager said as he went over to the cook... "Big order here!" he said as he rang the bell...

"You must be really hungry!" Wayne laughed...

"I am – but I really wanna make sure Starr and Chandler eat..."

"What about me?" he asked as he pulled me close to him and nibbled on my ear lobe...

"Yeesss..." I whispered as the manager came back over...

"Here's your food..." the manager said as he came over with two bags...

"Thanks..." Wayne said as he handed the manager his debit card. I took one of the bags as we waited for the manager to come back with the debit card...

"Here ya go – thanks again..."

"You're welcome..." Wayne said as he picked up the other bag and we left...

"Okay – let's go to the burger bar and get you a burger..." I said...

"Okay..." Wayne said as he smiled... "Ya know – I would've eaten the seafood..."

"I know – but I also know you really wanted a burger..." I said as we went inside...

"Welcome to Burger Bar..." the hostess said as we walked inside...

"Thank you..." I said...

"Would you like a table?"

"No thank you – we'll take an order to go..." I answered...

"Okay – what would you like?"

"I'd like two brisket burgers – with cheddar..." Wayne answered...

"Would you like fries with those burgers?"

"Yes Maam..."

"Honey – you gotta see this – they have kangaroo burgers!" I laughed...

"Sweetie – is it okay if I call you Sweetie?" Wayne asked...

"As long as your wife doesn't have a problem with it!" she laughed...

"Okay Sweetie – make that three brisket burgers with cheddar..."

"And fries?"

"And fries..." Wayne answered...

"Well done?"

"Well done..." Wayne answered...

"Okay – I'll be right back..." she said as she went to place the order...

"Honey – let's have some fun..." Wayne laughed...

"Okay – whatcha need me to do?"

"I'm gonna give Chandler a brisket burger... watch him eat it... then tell him he ate kangaroo..."

"Oh my God!" I laughed...

"You'll go along with it?"

"Hell yea!" I laughed...

"Can I get you something to drink while you wait?" the hostess asked...

"Yes – we'll have two long island iced teas..." Wayne answered...

"Honey – are you sure about that?" I laughed...

"We're not driving..."

"You're right..." I laughed...

"I'll be back with your drinks..." the hostess said as she went to get our drinks...

"I want us to come back here..." I said...

"We can..." Wayne said as he kissed me...

"I can't believe I'm here... with you..."

"Believe it..." he said as he kissed me again...

"I love you so much..."

"I love you too..."

"Are you newlyweds?" the hostess asked as she came with our drinks...

"Yes... we are..." Wayne answered as he took the drinks from her and handed me one...

"How long have you been married?"

"12 days..." Wayne answered...

"Aww... congratulations..."

"Thank you..." Wayne said as he raised his glass and I raised mine...

"To us..." I said...

"To us..." Wayne repeated and then we both took one sip... and then another... and then another... until our glasses were empty...

"Here's your burgers..." the hostess asked...

"Honey?"

"Yes Mary?"

"Call an Uber..." I laughed...

"Okay..." Wayne laughed as he handed the hostess his debit card...

"Mmmph... Mmmph... Mmmph... Mmmph... Mmmph!"

"Hmmph... Hmmph... Hmmph... Hmmph... Hmmph!"

"Damn..." Chandler breathed as he kissed her... "I'm glad you're feeling better...

"I feel wonderful..." she breathed...

"I'ma make a habit of staying in bed with you more often..." he breathed as he kissed her again...

"Feels good to me..." she breathed...

"We better get dressed..." he said as he kissed her again...

"Mmmm... why..."

"Because..." he said in between kisses... "Your parents..."

"We can... put... on... our... pajamas..."

"Okay..." Chandler breathed as he tried to get up but Starr pulled him back down... "Alright... you gin' get me started again..."

"But... I want... more..."

"Okay..." Chandler breathed as he eased himself back inside her and started thrusting...

"Hmmph...   Hmmph...   Hmmph... Hmmph..."

"Mmmph! Mmmph! Mmmph! Mmmph!"

"Chandler... stop..."

"Am I hurting you?"

"No – listen..."

"Starr? Chandler? You home?" I laughed...

"Oh shit – your parents!!" Chandler laughed as he got up...

"We're home – give us a sec..." Chandler said as he went to the bathroom, grabbed a washcloth, tossed it to Starr, and then grabbed one for himself...

"Hurry up – these bags are kinda heavy..." Wayne laughed...

"Chandler..." Starr whispered as they cleaned up and put on their pajamas...

"What?" he whispered back...

"They're drunk!" Starr laughed...

"Oh shit!" Chandler laughed...

"Open the door..." Wayne said...

"Okay..." Chandler laughed as he opened the door...

"Hey... Chandler..." Wayne laughed as he fell in the door and Chandler caught him...

"C'mon – sit down in the chair..." Chandler laughed as he helped Wayne sit down...

"Hey..." I laughed as I came in with the other bag...

"Hi Mommy..." Starr laughed as Chandler helped me sit in the chair...

"How you feelin'?" I asked as we took all the food out the bags...

"I'm fine – how are you?" she laughed...

"Drunk off my ass!" I laughed...

"I see..." Chandler laughed...

"C'mon – eat – we have burgers, fries, seafood platters, more fries, mac & cheese bites, cream cheese bites, and chicken fingers..." Wayne said...

"You and your burgers!" Chandler laughed...

"You like cheddar Chandler?" Wayne asked...

"Yea..."

"Good 'cause I got you a special burger from the Burger Bar... with cheddar cheese..." Wayne said as he handed Chandler the platter...

"I want the seafood platter, some mac & cheese bites, and some cream cheese bites..." Starr said as she helped herself...

"Me too..." I said as I helped myself along with her...

"Damn – this here good!" Chandler said...

"I told ya – I'm never wrong..." Wayne laughed as we ate...

"This is really good – what kinda burger is this?"

"Well... it's one of their specialities..." Wayne answered...

"It's real good – what is it?"

"Kangaroo..."

"Oh hell no! You gave me a damn kangaroo burger? Oh that's some bullshit!" I couldn't hold it in – I bust out laughing along with Wayne...

"Mommy! It's not funny!" Starr snapped...

"It's not kangaroo – it's brisket!" I laughed...

"Y'all didn't just give me kangaroo?" Chandler asked...

"Hell no!" Wayne laughed... "You really think I'd do that?"

"I'on know! That's what you said!"

"Chandler – its brisket – I promise..." Wayne laughed...

"I don't think that was funny..." Starr said...

"Yes the hell it was!" I laughed...

"It's cool – I can take a joke..." Chandler said...

"Well – at least I know I'm not eating kangaroo..." Starr said...

"No Baby – you're not..." I said...

"I'm gonna have the other burger – you wanna split it with me Chandler?" Wayne asked...

"Okay - sure..." Chandler laughed...

"Chandler – I ordered four platters – and I also ordered two platters of chicken fingers..." I said...

"Le'me get one of those..." Chandler said...

"Sure..." I said as I handed him a platter...

"I guess I'll take the other one..." Wayne said...

"I'm gonna eat another seafood platter... some more mac & cheese bites... and some more cream cheese puffs..." Starr said...

"Me too girl..." I said...

"So what are we doing for the rest of the day?" Chandler asked...

"I'ma go back to bed..." I yawned... "I need a nap..."

"We can do that..." Wayne said...

"We've been inside all day..." Starr said...

"What time is your train tomorrow?" Wayne asked...

"8:20 a.m." Chandler answered...

"What time do you get to the Canadian border?"

"10:22..."

"What time is the next train?"

"10:33..."

"What time will you get to new York?"

"9:59 p.m."

"Wow – that's a long ride – and then you have to go to Bridgeport after that?"

"Yea..."

"Hmmm... Mary – give me the laptop..."

"Okay..." I said as I passed him the laptop...

"What are you up to?" Chandler asked...

"Hang on a sec..." Wayne answered as he searched on his computer... "What time were you planning on getting up tomorrow?"

"7 o'clock – why?"

"If you can be ready at 4, I can get you to Niagara Falls in New York by 6:30 a.m. – you can get the 6:47 a.m. train to New York – you'll get there by 4:00 p.m. instead of 10:00 p.m."

"I don't wanna get up at 4:00 a.m. in the morning!" Starr whined..."

"Starr – we need to leave at 4:00 a.m...." Wayne said...

"4:00 a.m. is too early..." Chandler said...

"I know it's early – but you'll get to New York at 4:00 p.m. instead of 10:00 p.m. – you'll be back in Bridgeport before it gets dark – and you can sleep on the train..." Wayne said...

"I already bought the tickets..." Chandler said...

"You can change them – you call Amtrak – cancel the tickets you have – they'll issue a credit – you use the credit to purchase new tickets – if you have anything left over you can use the credit in the future – the credit doesn't expire..."

"I guess you've done this before..." Chandler laughed...

"I have..."

"Starr?"

"Yes Chandler?"

"It's up to you..."

"Okay..." she sighed...

"You know we leavin' at 4:00 in the morning – right?"

"Yea..."

"Okay – Wayne – let's do it..."

"Okay Chandler – pull up your reservation and cancel it – they'll send you an email with your credit – when you buy the new tickets you'll put the credit in..."

"Okay..." Chandler said as he sat down in front of the laptop..."

"I guess we better get to bed..." I said...

"Good thing we ate..." Starr yawned...

"You'll sleep through the night – I don't know about the rest of us though..." I laughed...

"I'm done – I just need to print these new tickets..." Chandler said...

"You can do that downstairs in the business center..." Wayne said...

"Okay – Starr – I'll be back…" Chandler said as he got up…

"I'm coming with you…"

"Starr – stay here – I'll be right back – I promise…"

"I'm not falling for that again…" Starr laughed…

"What's she talkin' about Chandler?" Wayne asked…

"Nothing…" Chandler laughed… "Okay Starr – you getting' dressed or you goin' in your pajamas?" Chandler asked…

"You said we're coming right back – I can just put on my robe and slippers…"

"Okay – we're going to our room – we'll see you downstairs at 3:30 a.m." Wayne said…

"3:30 a.m.? You said 4:00 a.m.!" Starr exclaimed…

"You need time to check out…" Wayne said…

"We don't need that much time – we'll just drop the key off and get ready…" Chandler laughed…

"Okay – c'mon Wayne – I need to go lay down…" I said as I stood up to leave…"

"Okay – see you in the morning…" Wayne said as he put his arm around me and we left the room…

Chapter 11

"Hello Conrad..."

"Hello Bazil..."

"How are you?"

"The tickets have been cancelled..."

"Tickets?"

"Your son-in-law cancelled their tickets..."

"Hmmm... - when we're they supposed to leave?"

"They were scheduled to leave tomorrow at 8:20 a.m."

"Maybe they're staying an extra day..."

"There's something else..."

"What is it Conrad?"

"He's been talking to Sergeant Hurley..."

"Oh yea – they went to the academy together..."

"He's been in communication with him quite a bit since he's been in Canada..."

"Should I be worried?"

"Naa...."

"Good..."

"I'll keep you posted..."

"Thank you Conrad..."

When we got in our room Wayne couldn't wait to close the door... "Take off your clothes..."

"Yes Daddy..." I squealed as I got undressed and stood in front of him. Wayne took off his clothes and stood in front of me fully erect. I looked him up and down and smiled as he just stood there. Wayne put his hand under his chin and I could tell he was deep in thought...

"What are you going to do to me?" I whispered. Wayne didn't answer me. He walked towards me, pulled me close to him, and held me as he looked in my eyes. I could feel his dick against me and when he tried to let go of me, I pulled him back towards me and kissed him. Wayne held me and kissed me back for a few moments and then he spoke...

"You know what happens when you rub my crotch in public?" he breathed in my ear...

"Yes Daddy..." I breathed...

"Come with me..." he commanded as he moved me over to the front of the dresser in front of the mirror. "Watch what I do to you..." he breathed as he stood behind me and began massaging my breasts...

"Oooohhh..." I moaned...

"Hmmm... your breasts feel fuller..." he breathed and then he started kissing me on my neck... "Don't close your eyes..." he commanded...

"Okay..." I breathed as I watched him continue to massage my breasts... "Ooohhh...."

"You like that?" he breathed...

"Yes Daddy..." I breathed. Wayne moved his hands down my stomach to my pelvis and held them there...

"Be still..." he whispered as he stopped me from moving. Wayne pushed his dick against my ass and I gasped... "You want this Mommy?" he breathed in my ear...

"Yes Daddy..." I breathed...

"Look how your chest is moving up and down..." he said as he moved his right hand down to my pussy, spread my lips, and started playing with my clit...

"Ooooohhh..." I moaned...

"Uh uh... open your eyes..." he commanded as he held his dick against my ass and continued playing with my clit...

"Huh... Daddy..." I moaned...

"Mmmm.... Yes Mommy..." he breathed as he slid his fingers inside me...

"Huh... Huh..."

"Mommy... you're so wet..." he breathed as he continued playing with my pussy with his right hand and began massaging my left breast with his left hand...

"Daddy... I'm gonna cum..." I moaned...

"Uh uh... not yet..." he commanded as he bent me forward and eased himself inside me...

"Oh Daddy... yes..." I moaned as he grabbed my waist and started thrusting...

"Your pussy feels good Mommy..."

"Ohhh... Ohhh... Ohhh..."

"Open your eyes..." he commanded as I braced myself on the dresser...

"Ooohhh... Ooohhh... Ooohhh..."

"Cum for Daddy..." he commanded as he fucked me harder...

"Ooohhh... Ooohhh... Ooohhh... Yes... Yes..."

"That's it Mommy... cum for me..."

"Huh! Huh! Huh! Huh! Huuuggghhhh!"

"Yes Mommy... was it good?" he breathed as he continued fucking me...

"Yes Daddy... yes..." I moaned...

"Good..." he breathed as he took his dick out my pussy and put it in my ass...

"Ooohhh..." I moaned as he started fucking my ass...

"Look at yourself..." he commanded as I looked in the mirror...

"Fuck me Daddy..." I moaned as I watched him fuck me...

"You like it Mommy?"

"I love it Daddy... Yes..."

"Mommy... I'm gonna cum..." he growled as he started fucking me harder...

"Fuck me Daddy... just like that..." I moaned...

"Ugh! Ugh! Ugh! Ugh!"

"Ha... Ha... Ha... Ha..."

"Uuuggghhhh!" Wayne held my waist and continued fucking my ass as I leaned forward and stopped looking in the mirror...

"Fuck... Daddy... I'm cumming!" I screamed. Wayne held on and continued fucking my ass as my legs trembled until my orgasm subsided and then Wayne took his dick out my ass and turned me around to face him... "I love you..." I said as I threw my arms around him...

"I love you too..." he breathed and then he kissed me...

"Let's go to bed..."

"Uh uh..." let's get in the shower..."

"Wayne... I'm tired..."

"So am I..." he said as he led me to the bathroom and turned on the shower.

Chapter 12

"Starr..." Chandler whispered as he kissed her awake...

"Yes Chandler..." she yawned...

"We need to get up..."

"I'm tired..."

"I know..."

"I don't want to go..."

"You can sleep in the car..."

"Okay..." she sighed as she got up and got out of bed...

"Here – put this on..." he said as he put an outfit on the bed for Starr to change into...

"I need to pack..."

"I did that already..."

"Thank you..." she yawned as she got dressed...

Give me your pajamas..." he said...

"Here..." she said as she stood up and handed him her pajamas. Chandler put them in the suitcase, closed it, put the suitcases by the door, went back over to the bed, pulled Starr up into his arms, and kissed her...

"Chandler... I have morning breath..."

"So do I..." he said as he kissed her again...

"Let's go..." she yawned..."

"Okay..."

"Mary..." Wayne whispered as he kissed me awake...

"Good morning..." I yawned...

"It's time to go..."

"What time is it?"

"It's 3:30..."

"Oh God – I need coffee..." I said as I got up out of bed...

"We'll get some on the way..." Wayne said as I started getting dressed. Wayne sat in the chair and smiled as he watched me get dressed...

"Okay – I'm ready..."

"Yes you are..." he said as he stood up and pulled me into a kiss...

"Wayne..."

"Yes Mary..." he answered and then he kissed me fully...

"I don't know how you do it..."

"Do what?"

"How are you so happy in the morning?"

"I woke up next to you..." he answered and then he kissed me again...

"I love you..."

"I love you too..."

"I can't wait to get back here..."

"Neither can I..." he breathed as he kissed me again...

"Let's go before I change my mind..." I laughed...

"Good morning!" Chandler beamed as we walked into the lobby...

"Good morning Chandler..." Wayne said...

"Morning..." I mumbled...

"Morning..." Starr yawned...

"You checked out?" Wayne asked...

"Yes sir!" Chandler answered...

"You have any coffee?"

"Yes sir!"

"Starr?"

"Yes Dad?"

"You have any coffee?"

"No..."

"C'mon Starr – let's get some coffee..." I said as I took Starr by the hand and led her into the dining area...

"You ready Chandler?" Wayne asked...

"I'm ready – thanks for doing this..."

"You're welcome..."

"We're ready..." I said as Starr and I walked into the lobby with our coffee...

"It's 3:50 a.m. – we're ahead of schedule – let's go..." Wayne said as we all went out to the parking lot, got in the car, and Wayne drove off. Starr finished her coffee and slept on Chandler's shoulder. I finished my coffee and looked out the window as Wayne drove. Chandler fell asleep but I stayed awake. Wayne would look over at me every so often and squeeze my hand. "We're here..." Wayne said after he parked the car...

"What time is it?" I asked...

"6:20 a.m." Wayne answered...

"Starr... we're here..." Chandler said as he woke her up...

"Okay..." she yawned. We all got out the car and went over to where everyone was waiting...

"I guess we're not the only one's..." Starr yawned...

"I guess not..." Chandler laughed...

"Attention passengers – the train going to Penn Station will be arriving shortly. Please have all tickets available for boarding...

"Bye Mommy..." Starr said as she pulled me into a hug...

"Bye Starr..." I said as I kissed her on her head...

"Bye Dad..." she said as he pulled Wayne into a hug...

"I love you Starr..." Wayne said...

"I love you too Dad..."

"Bye Mommy..." Chandler laughed as he pulled me into a hug...

"Bye Chandler..." I laughed...

"Bye Wayne..." Chandler said as he pulled Wayne into a hug...

"Bye Chandler..." Wayne said...

"I'm going to bug you until I get pictures..." I said...

"Pictures?" Chandler asked...

"I'm talking about my grandchild..." I answered...

"Or grandchildren..." Starr said...

"Hurry up and get me those pictures!" I said as the train pulled up and Starr started to cry...

"Don't cry Starr..." Wayne said as he pulled her into a hug...

"I'm gonna miss you..." she sniffed...

"We're just a train ride away..." I said. Chandler put the suitcases on the train and then came to get Starr...

"C'mon – we have to board the train..." he said as he took her hand... and Starr pulled away from him and grabbed onto me...

"Starr... we'll see you soon..."

"I don't wanna leave Mommy..."

"Starr... we'll see you soon... I promise..."

"Let's go!" the conductor yelled...

"C'mon Starr..." Chandler said...

"Okay..." she sighed as she let go of me, went with Chandler, and got on the train...

"Starr... what's wrong?" Chandler asked as he wiped her tears...

"I have a bad feeling..." she whispered...

"You okay?"

"Not me Chandler..."

"The baby?"

"No..."

"Starr... what is it?"

"It's Mommy…"

"I don't understand…"

"Remember our wedding night?"

"Of course!"

"Remember I said something was wrong with Beautiee?"

"Yea…"

"I felt it before we got married – I called Daddy and told him I was worried and he should stay close to her…"

"I didn't know that…"

'And my brother was born a month early…"

"Beautiee is fine and so is your brother…"

"Chandler!"

"Okay Starr…" Chandler said as he kissed her… "I'm listening – please stop crying…" he said as he held her and she put her head on his shoulder…

"I'm sorry…"

"What I tell you about apologizing?' he said as he lifted her head by her chin and kissed her…

"I love you…"

"I love you too – I'ma go get us some breakfast – I'll be right back…" he said as he got up…

"Okay…" Starr yawned…

"Hey Chandler…" Wayne answered…

"Can you talk?"

"We stopped to get breakfast before we get back on the road – how's Starr?"

"She's worried about her mother…"

"Oh boy…"

"She said she has a bad feeling…"

"I'll make Mary my priority…"

"Thank you – I'll call you when we get home…"

"Okay Chandler…"

"Is everything okay?"

"Yea…"

"Is Starr okay?"

"Mary?" Wayne asked as he took my hands…

"Yes Wayne?"

"Everything is okay… okay?"

"Okay…" I sighed…

"She's a lot like you…"

"Oh no you don't…" I laughed…

"Why are you so afraid to admit you're a sensitive?"

"I'm not afraid to admit anything!" I laughed…

"Okay… if you say so…" Wayne laughed…

"I'm not!"

"Okay, okay…" he laughed again…

"Maybe I am… a little…"

"So you admit it!"

"Don't you dare tell Starr I said that!"

"It'll be our secret…" he laughed as the waitress brought our food to the table and we ate breakfast…

"Where the hell you been?" Charles asked...

"Oh... hey Charles..." Chandler answered...

"Ya'll alright?" Theresa asked as she opened the door and came out into the hallway...

"Hey Tee... I'm fine... we're just tired..." Starr yawned...

"Where were you?" Charles asked...

"Charles... we need to go..." Chandler said as he opened the door and they went inside...

'Well damn!" Charles exclaimed...

"Charles... don't take it personal..." Theresa said...

"Why shouldn't I?"

"Charles – didn't you see how out of it Starr was?"

"I wasn't paying attention..."

"C'mon – I'll make us breakfast..." she said as she pulled Charles into a kiss...

"I love you baby..."

"I love you too..." she said as she pulled him in the door, closed it, and they continued kissing...

"I'm gonna sleep for a week!" Starr exclaimed as she stripped, went over to the bed, turned back the covers, got in bed, and pulled the covers up...

"Umm... Mrs. Corbett?"

"Yes Chandler?" she yawned...

"I'on know if I can let you go to sleep yet..." Chandler said as he stripped, went over to the bed, pulled the covers back, climbed in bed beside Starr, pulled the covers back up, and started kissing her...

"Chandler..." she whispered...

"Yes Starr..." he whispered between kisses...

"I'm so tired..."

"Just let me hold you..."

"Okay..." Starr yawned as she moved closer to Chandler and laid on his chest...

"It feels good to be home... in our bed..." Chandler yawned...

"It sure does..." Starr yawned as they both drifted off to sleep...

"Hello Conrad..."

"Hello Bazil..."

"How's everything?"

"They're home..."

"Thank you Conrad..."

Chapter 13

"Wayne..." I whispered...

"Yes Mary?"

"The phone's ringing..."

"Hello?" Wayne answered...

"Hello Wayne – its Vanessa..."

"Hi Vanessa..."

"I'm just calling to confirm our appointment for 9:00 a.m."

"We'll be downstairs at 9..."

"Could you be downstairs at 8?"

"Sure – we can be ready at 8..."

"I need to get you to the office to sign the papers at 9..."

"Okay Vanessa – we'll see you at 8..." Wayne said as he hung up...

"Everything okay?" I asked...

"Everything's fine..." Wayne answered as he kissed me...

"I can't wait..."

"Neither can I..."

"What time is it?"

"It's about 5..."

"They should be home now..."

"They are…"

"Maybe we should call them…"

"Maybe…" Wayne said as he took my face in his hands and kissed me… "We should…" he said and then he kissed me again… "Leave them… alone…"

"Mmmm… okay…" I breathed…

"Get dressed…"

"Okay…" I said as I jumped up out of bed and started getting dressed…

"In a bit of a hurry huh?" Wayne laughed as he got up and got dressed…

"It's just the two of us…"

"Yes it is…"

"I feel like we're back on our honeymoon…"

"Me too…" Wayne said as he pulled me into a kiss and held me…

"I love you…" I said as I threw my arms around his neck…

"I love you too…"

"Let's go!" I said excitedly…

"Aren't you going to ask me where we're going?"

"As long as I'm with you – I don't care!" I exclaimed as I took his hand and pulled him out the door towards the elevator…

"Mary… wait a sec…" Wayne laughed…

"I'm sorry… I can't help it…" I laughed as we got on the elevator and went to the lobby…

"You're so much like your daughter…" Wayne laughed…

"What?"

"You and Starr... you both act just alike when you're happy..." We went to the car, got it, and Wayne drove off. I looked out the window as we headed towards Victoria Avenue. We continued on Victoria Avenue for a while until Wayne turned onto Valley Way and then I saw it...

"The Moose and Petter Bistro!" I laughed...

"What's so funny?"

"If Chandler was here he'd tell us he ain't eatin' no damn moose!" I laughed...

"You're right!" Wayne laughed as he parked the car. We got out, went inside, and I started reading their philosophy statement on winning & dinning...

"Honey look – they want us to relax, sip some wine, and let the candlelight and jazz be our escape..."

"Sounds good..." Wayne said as we picked out a table and sat down...

"Welcome to the Moose and Petter Bistro – my name is Heather – may I start you off with something to drink?"

"What's on your Date Night Menu?" Wayne asked...

"Oh I'm sorry – you're on a date?"

"We're actually on our honeymoon..." I answered...

"Congratulations! How long have you been married?"

"13 days..." I sighed...

"Aww... that's nice – let's see – on the Date Night Menu we have the Riesling Vidal or Gamay Merlot – which bottle would you prefer?"

"The Gamay Merlot..." Wayne answered as he took my hand...

"Okay – would you like onion soup, garden salad, bruschetta bread, or cheese bread?"

"Garden salad..." Wayne answered...

"And for you sweetie?" she asked me...

"Garden salad..." I answered...

"Okay – for your main course we have chicken parmesan with spaghetti, spinach cheese ravioli, sausage and pepper penne, breaded schnitzel with lemon served with garlic butter noodles, and braciole – flank steak rolled with ground pork and herbs, topped with mushroom pepper sauce with mashed potato and vegetable medley..."

"I'll have the chicken parmesan..." I said...

"I'll have the braciole..." Wayne said...

"Okay – for dessert we have crème brulee, pumkin cake, or mocha fudge brownie pie..."

"Mocha fudge brownie pie..." we both said in unison...

"Okay! I'll be back with your wine..." Heather said as she went to get our wine...

"How'd you find this place?" I asked...

"I googled it..."

"I'm surprised we didn't find it when Chandler was here..."

"I'm glad we didn't..."

"Me too..."

"Here's your wine..." heather said as she put the wine on the table along with our glasses. Heather opened the bottle and poured the wine as the jazz music began playing in the background... "I'll be back with your salads..." she said as she walked away...

"Here's to my beautiful wife..." Wayne said as he lifted his glass...

"To your beautiful wife..." I acknowledged as we both took a sip...

"Here's to my fine husband..." I said as I raised my glass...

"To your fine husband..." Wayne acknowledged as we both took another sip...

"Here's your salads..." Heather said as she placed our salads on the table...

"In 13 days my life has taken a wild, crazy turn..." I said...

"So has mine..." Wayne said...

"You are everything I ever wanted..."

"Mary..." Wayne whispered as he started to cry... "I love you so much..."

"I love you too..." I said as I got up from my side of the booth, sat beside Wayne, and pulled him into a hug...

"Aww..." Heather said as she came back to the table with our food...

"This looks good... let's eat..." Wayne said...

"Okay…" I said. I got up and sat back down across from Wayne and we sipped wine, ate, and listened to jazz music. Heather came back and forth a few times to check on us and the other guests. Everyone was smiling, talking, and enjoying the music…

"Are you ready for dessert?" Heather asked as she came to the table to gather our plates…

"Yea…" we both said in unison…

"Okay – I'll be back with your dessert…" she said as she walked away…

"We need to come back here…" Wayne said…

"Yes we do…" I agreed…

"How'd you like Date Night once a week?"

"I'd love it…"

"Here's your dessert…" heather said as she put our mocha fudge brownie pies on the table…

"Mmmm…." Wayne said as he tasted his dessert…

"Ooohhh… this is good…" I breathed as I tasted mine. We ate our dessert without speaking…

"Are you ready for the check?" Heather asked…

"We're ready…" we both said in unison…

"I'll be right back with your check…" she said as she went to get our check. When she came back to the table with the check Wayne put the debit card in the check holder without even looking at it. Heather picked it up and brought it right back to the table for Wayne to sign...

"You ready to go?" Wayne asked...

"Yea..." I sighed...

"Let's go..." Wayne said as he stood up and extended his hand. I took his hand, stood up, and we went to get in the car and headed back to the hotel...

"Hey Chandler..." Wayne answered as he put the phone on speaker...

"Hey Wayne – we're home!"

"I knew that..." Wayne laughed... "So how was your trip?"

"It was long – but we slept most of the way – and we went to sleep as soon as we got in – we just woke up..."

"We woke up around 5..." I laughed...

"Hi Mommy!"

"Hi Starr – how are you feeling?"

"Wonderful..."

"Aww..." Wayne and I both said in unison...

"Hi Dad..."

"Hi Starr..."

"How are you?"

"I'm great – your Mom and I just got back from our date..."

"Aww... how sweet..."

"You goin' to work tomorrow Starr?" I asked...

"Naa… I'm still tired… and hungry!" Starr laughed…

"We're gonna go now – we gotta get up early…" I said…

"That's right – y'all close tomorrow…" Chandler said…

"Yes we do…" Wayne said…

"Good night – love you…" Starr said…

"Good night – love you too…" I said…

"Good night Chandler – good night kid – love you…" Wayne said…

"Good night Dad – love you too…"

"Good night Chandler – love you…" I said…

"Good night – love y'all too…" Chandler said as he hung up…

"Chandler? You up?" Charles asked as he banged on the door…

"Hold on!" Chandler snapped as he opened the door…

"Listen – my wife made cheese burgers and fries – y'all hungry?"

"I'm hungry!" Starr yelled out from the bedroom…

"We'll be there in a few minutes…" Chandler laughed…

"Okay – see you then…" Charles said as he went back to his apartment…

"You ready Starr?" Chandler asked…

"I'm ready..." Starr answered as she came out in her pajamas, her robe, and slippers...

"That's how you gin' over there?" Chandler laughed...

"Uh huh..." Starr answered as she opened the door and held it for Chandler...

"Are they comin'?" Theresa asked...

"Yea babe..."

"Good – we gotta feed 'em first – then we can be nosy..." she laughed...

"I love you..." Charles said as he pulled her into a kiss...

"I love you too..."

"You think they'll be fuckin' later?"

"Charles!"

"Well... do you?"

"I'on know!" she laughed...

"I hope so – I like when we all get it in together..."

"You are so bad!" she laughed...

"You love it when I'm bad..." Charles growled in her ear as he began massaging her breasts..."

"Charles..." she moaned. Charles ran his hands down her stomach, opened her robe, slid her panties to the side, and slipped his finger inside her... "Charles..." she whispered...

"I'ma tear your pussy up after they leave..." he said as he started playing with her clit...

"Charles – its Chandler... they're at the door..." she panted...

"Cum for me..." he growled in her ear as he rubbed her clit faster...

"Charles... oh God..."

"Yes... that's it..."

"Charles... Charles... Charles..."

"Your pussy's so wet..." he growled in her ear...

"Charles... I'm cumming..." she panted as her legs trembled...

"Yes baby... give it to Daddy..." he growled in her ear...

"Shit..." she panted... "I want you to fuck me now Daddy..."

"Soon as they go home..." he growled in her ear... "I'm gonna fuck the shit outta you..." Theresa closed her robe, tied it, and went to open the door...

"Come on in guys..." she panted...

"Y'all good?" Chandler asked as they came in...

"We're good..." Charles answered as he licked his fingers and smiled at Theresa mischievously...

"Smells good!" Starr exclaimed as she sat at the table...

"It is..." Theresa said as she put a plate of eight cheeseburgers on the table along with a pan of fries, a spatula, and extra plates...

"Listen here – we home now – y'all gotta let us cook for you next..." Chandler said as he sat at the table...

"Oh my God – this is so good!" Starr exclaimed as she ate...

"When was the last time you ate?" Theresa asked...

"About 7:00 a.m."

"Oh my God! Starr! You can't do that! You're pregnant! Why aren't you eating?"

"I was sleep most of the day..."

"That's it – I'm taking you to my doctor – you shouldn't be that tired!"

"Babe – calm down..." Charles said...

"Charles – it isn't right!"

"Theresa – I know you mean well – but Starr's okay..." Chandler said...

"Is she?" Theresa asked...

"Babe... calm down..." Charles said as he took her hand and kissed it... "Please..."

"We lost our baby last year..." Theresa said...

"Oh wow... I'm sorry..." Starr said...

"No... I'm sorry – I didn't mean to get so worked up..." Theresa said...

"I'ma tell you the same thing I tell my wife – stop apologizing..." Chandler said...

"Stop apologizing?" Charles asked...

"You don't have to apologize for your feelings..." Chandler answered...

"Oh okay... you right..." Charles said...

"If you wrong – you apologize – but if you're hurt, sad, mad – whatever – you don't need to apologize for that…" Chandler said…

"Alright, alright – we heard you…" Charles laughed…

"Are you gonna try again?" Starr asked…

"We've been trying every day since… never mind…" Theresa answered…

"Since you heard us on the balcony?" Starr asked…

"Yea…"

"Chandler – where the hell y'all been?" Charles asked…

"Starr's parents moved to Ontario…"

"Canada?"

"Yea…"

"So that's where y'all were?"

"Yea…"

"So that morning when I saw you – why couldn't you tell me?"

"Her parents had a situation – the police met them at the train – we had to go see about them…"

"Oh damn – sorry to hear that – they good?"

"They're fine…" Starr sighed…

"Starr?"

"Yes Theresa?"

"Why didn't you eat today?"

"We got up at 3:30 this morning to make a 6:30 train – we were supposed to leave at 8:20

a.m. but my Dad drove us to Niagara Falls so we could get home before midnight…"

"Oh wow! No wonder you're so tired – but you need to eat – even if that means Chandler has to wake you up to feed you…"

"Or you can wake me up and feed me…" Starr laughed…

"So did you stay with her parents?" Charles asked…

"We all stayed in a hotel…" Chandler answered…

"They don't have a place yet?"

"They close tomorrow…" Starr answered…

"So wait – they moved up there – and didn't have anywhere to stay?" Charles asked…

"They had a situation – they good now…" Chandler answered…

"Okay – I'ma stop askin'…" Charles laughed…

"Starr – are you working tomorrow?" Theresa asked…

"Naaa…"

"Good – I'm taking you to my doctor…"

"Does she deliver babies?"

"Yea…"

"Where is she?"

"She's here in Bridgeport…"

"Okay…"

"What time we need to be ready?" Chandler asked…

"Eight o'clock…" Theresa answered…

"Okay..." Chandler said...

"Y'all thirsty?" Charles asked...

"I'm thirsty..." Starr answered...

"We got ginger ale and Pepsi..." Theresa said...

"I'll take ginger ale..." Starr said...

"Oh shoot – I forgot – Charles had the last Pepsi – we only have ginger ale..." Theresa said...

"That's fine..." Chandler said...

When we got in the room, Wayne couldn't wait to close the door... "Mrs. Robinson..." he breathed as he pushed me up against the door and kissed me hard...

"Yes... Mr. Robinson?" I breathed...

"You..." he said as he kissed me again... "Have... made... me... the... happiest... man... in... the... world..."

"Are... you... going... to... reward... me... or... punish... me?"

"Depends... on... what... you... want..."

"Mmmm... both..."

"Okay..." he breathed as he took me over to the bed and began undressing me... "First... I'll punish you... then I'll reward you..."

"C'mon Starr – I need to make sure you get plenty of rest..." Chandler said as he got up to leave...

"Okay..." Starr said as she stretched and then got up...

"Y'all just gonna eat and run huh?" Charles laughed...

"It's Sunday man – if you want us to spend the night, you gotta invite us over on Saturday..." Chandler laughed...

"Okay..." Charles laughed...

"I'll cook something tomorrow..." Starr said...

"Can you cook?" Theresa laughed...

"We'll find out tomorrow..." Starr laughed...

"Watcha cookin'?" Charles asked...

"A lil' bit of this, a lil' bit of that..." Starr answered...

"Okay!" We'll see you tomorrow!" Charles exclaimed...

"Good night – and thanks for dinner..." Chandler said...

"Good night – see you tomorrow..." Charles said as he damn near pushed them out the door...

"Whew – now I can clean this kitchen..." Theresa said...

"Guess again..." Charles said as he grabbed her from behind...

"Charles..."

"Yes..." he answered as he opened her robe and stuck his hand inside her panties. Theresa didn't answer him. She led him to the bedroom, turned to face him, and fell backwards on the bed with Charles falling down on top of her...

"Mrs. Corbett?" Chandler asked as they went inside and closed the door...

"Yes Mr. Corbett?" Starr answered as she threw her arms around Chandler's neck, lifter her legs, and wrapped them around Chandler's waist...

"Time for dessert..." he said as he carried her into the bedroom, laid her down on the bed, and laid down on top of her...

"Haa.... Haa.... Haa..."

"You wanted to be punished right?" Wayne growled...

"Yes... oh God... Yes..." I moaned as Wayne fucked me from behind...

"Uggh! Uggh! Uggh! Uggh!"

"Haa! Haa! Haa! Haa!

"Uggh!   Uggh!   Uggh!   Uggh! Uuuugggghhhh!"

"Aagh! Aagh! Aagh! Aagh! Aaaggghhhh!" I collapsed on my stomach and Wayne collapsed on top of me...

"What did I tell you I was going to do to you when they went home?" Charles breathed as he removed Theresa's panties and tossed them to the floor...

"You said you were going to fuck the shit outta me..." she breathed as he eased himself inside her and started thrusting...

"Charles... Oh yes..."

"Chandler... huh... huh... huh..."

"Umph... Umph... Umph..." Starr spread her legs wider, pulled Chandler down on top of her, and kissed him hard as Chandler thrust his tongue in her mouth... Hmmph... Hmmph... Hmmph... Hmmph...Hmmphhhh!"

"Ummph... Ummph... Ummph... Ummph... Ummphhhh!"

"Mary..." Wayne whispered...

"Yes..."

"It's time..."

"What time is it?"

"It's 7 o'clock..."

"Oh shoot!" I exclaimed as I jumped up out of bed...

"I guess you're excited..." Wayne laughed...

"Ya think?" I laughed as I rant to the bathroom and turned on the shower...

"Don't start without me..." Wayne said as he stepped into the shower with me...

"Starr..." Chandler whispered as he kissed her in her ear...

"Good morning..." she said and then she turned to face him...

"Good morning..." he said and then he kissed her...

"Mmmm... it feels so good to be in our bed again..."

"I wish we could stay here... but we can't..."

"I'm just happy to be home..."

"Me too..."

"I can't wait to go to the doctor..."

"Really? You're not nervous?"

"I am – but I'm more happy than nervous..." she said as she got up out of bed and stood in front of Chandler...

"C'mere..." Chandler said as he stood up, pulled Starr to him, and kissed her...

"Mmmm... what's that for?"

"I love you..."

"I love you too Chandler..."

"Let's go get in the shower..." he breathed as he kissed her again...

"Okay... but be can't do anything else... I wanna be ready on time..."

"So..." he asked as he pressed his erection against her... "You don't want me?"

"Chandler..." she laughed as she threw her arms around him and kissed him...

"Charles..." Theresa whispered...

"Good morning..." he yawned...

"You workin' today?"

"Yea..."

"I'ma go get in the shower right quick so I can take Starr to see LuAnn..." she said as she went to get up... and Charles pulled her back down, got on top of her, and eased himself inside her...

"Charles..." she moaned...

"Yeesss...."

"I can't believe we're getting our keys today!" I exclaimed as I started getting dressed...

"I can't wait..." Wayne said as he pulled me into a kiss...

"Let's go downstairs and have breakfast – I need to make sure my stomach isn't growling while we're sitting there..." I said as I took Wayne's hand and pulled him towards the door...

"Mary..."

"Yes Wayne?"

"Wait a minute..." he said as he pulled me into a kiss...

"Wayne..."

"Let's just get coffee – we can go out to celebrate after we sign the papers and get our keys..."

"Okay..." I said as we left the room. When we got to the lobby we headed straight for the dining room and I got us a table...

"I'll go get us some coffee..." Wayne said as he went to get us coffee. I looked around as I sat there waiting. It felt strange being just the two of us again but it felt nice...

"Where were you just then?" Wayne asked as he sat down...

"I was just thinking…" I sighed as I started drinking my coffee…

"About what?"

"It feels strange not having Starr and Chandler with us…"

"You miss them?"

"Yea…"

"Me too…"

"But I'm glad we're back on our honeymoon…"

"Me too…"

"Happy Anniversary…"

"Happy Anniversary…" Wayne said and then he kissed me…

"I can't believe it's only been two weeks…"

"I know…"

"If anybody told me this is where I was going to wind up…"

"Yea?"

"Yea…" I sighed…

"I don't want us to check out yet…"

"You don't?"

"Nope…"

"Why not?"

"I want us to clean it up, go shopping, pull up the carpet, and have new floors installed…"

'All I need is that bed you promised me – I can wait on everything else…" I laughed…

"You'll get your bed – but I want everything done before I start work…"

"I don't want to stay in the hotel after we get our keys..."

"Mary – I know you want to move in – but I want a chance to make it nice before we do..."

"Okay..." I sighed...

"Never mind – we can move in today if you want..."

"We can? Really"

"Sure... if that's what you really want..."

"I want it, I want it, I want it!" I laughed...

"Have a great day..." Theresa said as she kissed Charles...

"You too..."

"I'm sorry I can't make you coffee..."

"What'd Chandler tell you about apologizing?" he laughed...

"That's not what he meant..." she laughed...

"I'll stop and get coffee at Dunkin' Donuts..."

"I'll make it up to you..."

"You already have..." he said as he pulled her into a kiss...

"Charles..." she breathed...

"Let me know what the doctor says..." he said as he went towards the door, opened it, and waited for her...

"I will Charles..." she said as she ran right into Starr... literally...

"Ooopppsss!" Starr laughed...

"Oh my God – I'm sorry!" Theresa laughed...

"Good morning – see y'all later..." Charles said as he went to the elevator, got in, and closed the door...

"He in a hurry?" Chandler laughed...

"Yea..." Theresa laughed...

"Let's go..." Starr said...

"You nervous?" Theresa asked...

"Kinda..."

"You'll be fine..." Theresa said as they went to the elevator, got in, and went downstairs...

"I know..." Starr said as she squeezed Chandler's hand...

"My car... or yours?" Theresa asked...

"We'll follow you..." Chandler said...

"Okay..." Theresa said as she went to her car and got in...

"C'mon Starr..." Chandler said as he took her by the hand, escorted her to the car, opened the door for her, and waited for her to get in. After she got in he closed the door, went around to the driver's side, got in, and started the car...

"Chandler – Theresa's pulling out..." Starr said...

"Okay..." Chandler said as he pulled out behind her and followed her to Dr. Russo's office...

Twisted Mary Tree

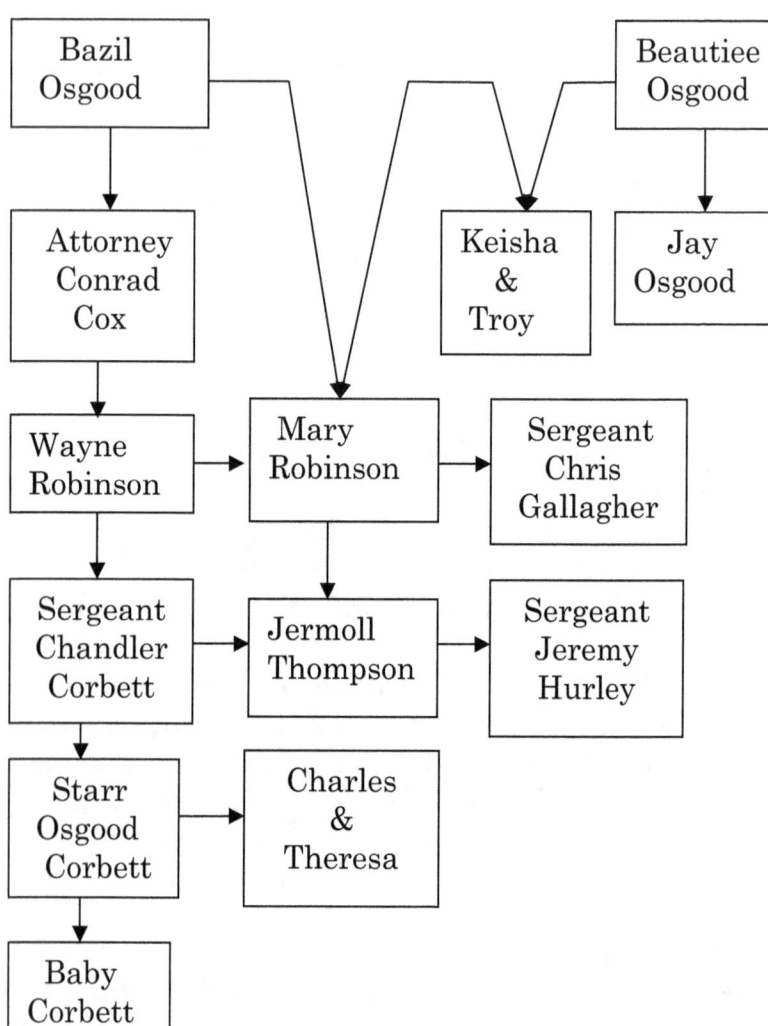